AMSTERDAM

Ian McEwan has written two collections of stories, *First Love, Last Rites* and *In Between the Sheets*, and seven novels, *The Cement Garden, The Comfort of Strangers, The Child in Time, The Innocent, Black Dogs, The Daydreamer* and *Enduring Love*. He has also written several film scripts, including *The Imitation Game, The Ploughman's Lunch, Sour Sweet, The Good Son* and *The Innocent*.

BY IAN McEWAN

First Love, Last Rites

In Between the Sheets

The Cement Garden

The Comfort of Strangers

The Child in Time

The Innocent

Black Dogs

The Daydreamer

Enduring Love

The Imitation Game
(plays for television)

Or Shall We Die?
(libretto for oratorio by Michael Berkeley)

The Ploughman's Lunch
(film script)

Sour Sweet
(film script)

'As ever, the McEwan plot is a finely tuned mechanism set to detonate from the first chapter'
Terence Blacker, *Mail on Sunday*

'The novel twists and turns unexpectedly...*Amsterdam* is an enigma...The narrative pivots on mystery and a blinding last-chapter revelation. On the way, the reader can relish the black tints of the prose...McEwan has a master's control over his instrument'
John Sutherland, *Sunday Times*

'Within only a few pages of *Enduring Love*, *Black Dogs* and *The Child in Time*, McEwan crisply sets up a haunting dramatic situation that will have repercussions throughout the book. We sense the author skilfully lighting his fuse and are compelled to find out just how it will explode. *Amsterdam* is no exception'
Alain de Botton, *Independent on Sunday*

Ian McEwan

AMSTERDAM

V

VINTAGE

Published by Vintage 1999

4 6 8 10 9 7 5 3

First published in Great Britain in 1998
by Jonathan Cape

Vintage
Random House, 20 Vauxhall Bridge Road,
London SW1V 2SA

Random House Australia (Pty) Limited
20 Alfred Street, Milsons Point, Sydney
New South Wales 2061, Australia

Random House New Zealand Limited
18 Poland Road, Glenfield,
Auckland 10, New Zealand

Random House South Africa (Pty) Limited
Endulini, 5A Jubilee Road, Parktown 2193, South Africa

The Random House Group Limited Reg. No 954009
www.randomhouse.co.uk

A CIP catalogue record for this book
is available from the British Library

ISBN 0 09 928957 1

Papers used by Random House are natural,
recyclable products made from wood grown in sustainable
forests. The manufacturing processes conform to the
environmental regulations of the country of origin

Printed and bound in Great Britain by
Cox & Wyman, Reading, Berkshire

TO JACO AND ELISABETH GROOT

The friends who met here and embraced are gone,
Each to his own mistake;

W.H. Auden, 'The Crossroads'

I

I

i

Two former lovers of Molly Lane stood waiting outside the crematorium chapel with their backs to the February chill. It had all been said before, but they said it again.

'She never knew what hit her.'

'When she did it was too late.'

'Rapid onset.'

'Poor Molly.'

'Mmm.'

Poor Molly. It began with a tingling in her arm as she raised it outside the Dorchester Grill to stop a cab; a sensation that never went away. Within weeks she was fumbling for the names of things. *Parliament, chemistry, propeller* she could forgive herself, but less so *bed, cream, mirror*. It was after the temporary disappearance of *acanthus* and *bresaiola* that she sought medical advice, expecting reassurance. Instead, she was sent for tests and, in a sense, never returned. How quickly feisty Molly became the sick-room prisoner of her morose, possessive husband, George. Molly, restaurant critic, gorgeous wit and photographer, the daring gardener who had been loved by the Foreign Secretary and could still turn a perfect cartwheel at the age of forty-six. The speed of her descent into madness and pain became a matter of common gossip: the loss of control of bodily function and with it all sense of humour, and then the tailing off into vagueness interspersed with episodes of ineffectual violence and muffled shrieking.

It was the sight now of George emerging from the chapel that caused Molly's lovers to move off further up the weedy gravel path. They wandered into an arrangement of oval rose beds, marked by a sign, 'The Garden of Remembrance'. Each plant had been savagely cut back to within a few inches of the frozen ground, a practice Molly used to deplore. The patch of lawn was strewn with flattened cigarette butts, for this was a place where people came to stand about and wait for the funeral party ahead of theirs to clear the building. As they strolled up and down, the two old friends resumed the conversation they had had in various forms a half dozen times before but which gave them rather more comfort than singing 'Pilgrim'.

Clive Linley had known Molly first, back when they were students in '68 and lived together in a chaotic, shifting household in the Vale of Health.

'A terrible way to go.'

He watched his own vaporised breath float off into the grey air. The temperature in central London was said to be minus eleven today. Minus eleven. There was something seriously wrong with the world for which neither God nor his absence could be blamed. Man's first disobedience, the Fall, a falling figure, an oboe, nine notes, ten notes. Clive had the gift of perfect pitch and heard them descending from the G. There was no need to write them down.

He continued, 'I mean, to die that way, with no

awareness, like an animal. To be reduced, humiliated before she could make arrangements, or even say goodbye. It crept up on her, and then . . .'

He shrugged. They came to the end of the trampled lawn, turned and walked back.

'She would have killed herself rather than end up like that,' Vernon Halliday said. He had lived with her for a year in Paris in '74 when he had his first job with Reuters and Molly did something or other for *Vogue*.

'Brain-dead and in George's clutches,' Clive said.

George, the sad, rich publisher who doted on her and whom, to everyone's surprise, she had not left, though she always treated him badly. They looked now to where he stood outside the door, receiving commiseration from a group of mourners. Her death had raised him from general contempt. He appeared to have grown an inch or two, his back had straightened, his voice had deepened, a new dignity had narrowed his pleading, greedy eyes. Refusing to consign her to a home, he had cared for her with his own hands. More to the point, in the early days when people still wanted to see her, he vetted her visitors. Clive and Vernon were strictly rationed because they were considered to make her excitable and, afterwards, depressed about her condition. Another key male, the Foreign Secretary, was also unwelcome. People began to mutter, there were muted references in a couple of gossip columns. And then it no longer mattered because the word was she was horribly not herself; people didn't want to go and see her and were glad that George was there to prevent them. Clive and Vernon, however, continued to enjoy loathing him.

As they turned about again, the phone in Vernon's pocket rang. He excused himself and stepped aside, leaving his friend to proceed alone. Clive drew his overcoat about him and slowed his pace. There must have been over two hundred in the black-suited crowd outside the crematorium now. Soon it would seem rude not to go over and say something to George. He got her finally, when she couldn't recognise her own face in the mirror. He could do nothing about her affairs, but in the end she was entirely his. Clive was losing the sensation in his feet, and as he stamped them the rhythm gave him back the ten note falling figure, ritardando, a cor anglais, and rising softly against it, contrapuntally, cellos in mirror image. Her face in it. The end. All he wanted now was the warmth, the silence of his studio, the piano, the unfinished score, and to reach the end. He heard Vernon say in parting, 'Fine. Rewrite the standfirst and run it on page four. I'll be there in a couple of hours.' Then he said to Clive, 'Bloody Israelis. We ought to wander over.'

'I suppose so.'

But instead they took another turn about the lawn for they were there, after all, to bury Molly.

With a visible effort of concentration, Vernon resisted the anxieties of his office. 'She was a lovely girl. Remember the snooker table.'

In 1978 a group of friends rented a large house in Scotland for Christmas. Molly and the man she was going about with at the time, a QC named Brady, staged an

Adam and Eve tableau on a disused snooker table, he in his Y-fronts, she in bra and panties, a cue rest for a snake and a red ball for an apple. The story handed down, however, the one that had appeared in an obituary and was remembered that way even by some who were present, was that Molly 'danced naked on Christmas Eve on a snooker table in a Scottish castle'.

'A lovely girl,' Clive repeated.

She had looked right at him when she pretended to bite the apple, and smiled raunchily through her chomping, with one hand on a jutting hip, like a music hall parody of a tart. He thought it was a signal, the way she held his gaze, and sure enough, they were back together that April. She moved into the studio in South Kensington and stayed through the summer. This was about the time her restaurant column was taking off, when she went on television to denounce the Michelin guide as the 'kitsch of cuisine'. It was also the time of his own first break, the *Orchestral Variations* at the Festival Hall. Second time round. She probably hadn't changed, but he had. Ten years on he'd learned enough to let her teach him something. He'd always been of the hammer and tongs school. She taught him sexual stealth, the occasional necessity of stillness. Lie still, like this, look at me, really look at me. We're a time bomb. He was almost thirty, by today's standards a late developer. When she found a place of her own and packed her bags he asked her to marry him. She kissed him, and quoted in his ear, *He married a woman to stop her getting away / Now she's there all day.* She was right, for when she went he was happier than ever

7

to be alone and wrote the *Three Autumn Songs* in less than a month.

'Did you ever learn anything from her?' Clive asked suddenly.

In the mid-eighties Vernon too had had a second bite, on holiday on an estate in Umbria. Then he was Rome correspondent for the paper he now edited, and a married man.

'I can never remember sex,' he said after a pause. 'I'm sure it was brilliant. But I do remember her teaching me all about porcini, picking them, cooking them.'

Clive assumed this was an evasion and decided against any confidences of his own. He looked over towards the chapel entrance. They would have to go across. He surprised himself by saying rather savagely, 'You know, I should have married her. When she started to go under I would have killed her with a pillow or something and saved her from everyone's pity.'

Vernon was laughing as he steered his friend away from the Garden of Remembrance. 'Easily said. I can just see you writing exercise-yard anthems for the cons, like what's her name, the suffragette.'

'Ethel Smyth. I'd do a damn better job than she did.'

The friends of Molly who made up the funeral gathering would have preferred not to be at a crematorium, but George had made it clear there was to be no memorial service. He didn't want to hear these three former lovers publicly comparing notes from the pulpits of St Martin's or St James's, or exchanging glances while he made his own speech. As Clive and Vernon approached they heard the familiar gabble of a cocktail party. No champagne trays, no restaurant walls to throw back the sound, but otherwise one might have been at one more gallery opening, one more media launch. So many faces Clive had never seen by daylight, and looking terrible, like cadavers jerked upright to welcome the newly dead. Invigorated by this jolt of misanthropy, he moved sleekly through the din, ignored his name when it was called, withdrew his elbow when it was plucked, and kept on going towards where George stood talking to two women and a shrivelled old cove with a fedora and stick.

'It's too cold, we have to go,' Clive heard a voice cry out, but for the moment no one could escape the centripetal power of a social event. He had already lost Vernon, who had been pulled away by the owner of a television channel.

At last Clive was gripping George's hand in a reasonable display of sincerity. 'It was a wonderful service.'

'It was very kind of you to come.'

Her death had ennobled him. The quiet gravity really wasn't his style at all, which had always been both needy and dour; anxious to be liked, but incapable of taking friendliness for granted. A burden of the hugely rich.

'And do excuse me,' he added, 'these are the Finch sisters, Vera and Mini, who knew Molly from her Boston days. Clive Linley.'

They shook hands.

'You're the composer?' Vera or Mini asked.

'That's right.'

'It's a great honour, Mr Linley. My eleven-year-old

granddaughter studied your sonatina for her grade exam in violin and really loved it.'

'That's very nice to know.'

The thought of children playing his music made him feel faintly depressed.

'And this,' George said, 'also from the States, is Hart Pullman.'

'Hart Pullman. At last. Do you remember I set your *Rage* poems for jazz orchestra?'

Pullman was the Beat poet, the last survivor of the Kerouac generation. He was a withered little lizard of a man who was having trouble twisting his neck to look up at Clive. 'These days I don't remember a thing, not a fucking thing,' he said pleasantly in a high-pitched, chirpy voice. 'But if you said you did it, you did it.'

'You remember Molly, though,' Clive said.

'Who?' Pullman kept a straight face for two seconds, then cackled and clutched at Clive's forearm with slender white fingers. 'Oh sure,' he said in his Bugs Bunny voice, 'Molly and me go way back to 'sixty-five in the East Village. I remember Molly. Oh boy!'

Clive concealed his disquiet as he did the sums. She would have turned sixteen in the June of that year. Why had she never mentioned it? He probed neutrally.

'She came out for the summer, I suppose.'

'Uh uh. She came to my Twelfth Night party. What a girl, eh George?'

Statutory rape then. Three years before him. She never told him about Hart Pullman. And didn't she come to the première of *Rage*? Didn't she come to the restaurant afterwards? He couldn't remember. Not a fucking thing.

George had turned his back to talk to the American sisters. Deciding there was nothing to lose, Clive cupped his hand about his mouth and leaned down to speak in Pullman's ear.

'You never fucked her, you lying reptile. She wouldn't have stooped to it.'

It wasn't his intention to walk away at this point, for he wanted to hear Pullman's reply, but just then two loud groups cut in from left and right, one to pay respects to George, the other to honour the poet, and in a swirl of repositioning Clive found himself freed and walking away. Hart Pullman and the teenage Molly. Sickened, he pushed his way back through the crowd and arrived in a small clearing and stood there, mercifully ignored, looking around at the friends and acquaintances absorbed in conversation. He felt himself to be the only one who really missed Molly. Perhaps if he'd married her he would have been worse than George, and wouldn't even have tolerated this gathering. Nor her helplessness. Tipping from the little, squarish brown plastic bottle, thirty sleeping pills into his palm. The pestle and mortar, a tumbler of scotch. Three tablespoons of yellow-white sludge. She looked at him when she took it, as if she knew. With his left hand he cupped her chin to catch the spill. He held her while she slept, and then all through the night.

Nobody else was missing her. He looked around at his fellow mourners now, many of them his own age, Molly's age, to within a year or two. How prosperous, how influential, how they had flourished under a government they had despised for almost seventeen years. *Talking 'bout my generation.* Such energy, such luck. Nurtured in the post-war settlement with the State's own milk and juice, and then sustained by their parents' tentative, innocent prosperity, to come of age in full employment, new universities, bright paperback books, the Augustan age of rock and roll, affordable ideals. When the ladder crumbled behind them, when the State withdrew her tit and became a scold, they were already safe, they consolidated, and settled down to forming this or that – taste, opinion, fortunes.

He heard a woman call out merrily, 'I can't feel my hands or feet and I'm going!' As he turned he saw a young man behind him who had been about to touch his shoulder. He was in his mid-twenties, and bald, or shorn, and wore a grey suit with no overcoat.

'Mr Linley. I'm sorry to intrude on your thoughts,' the man said, drawing his hand away.

Clive assumed he was a musician, or someone come to collect his autograph, and shrank his face into its mask of patience. 'That's all right.'

'I was wondering if you'd have time to come across and talk to the Foreign Secretary. He's keen to meet you.'

Clive pursed his lips. He didn't want to be introduced to Julian Garmony, but nor did he want to go to the bother of snubbing him. No escape. 'You show the way,' he said, and was led past standing clumps of his friends, some of whom guessed where he was going and tried to lure him from his guide.

'Hey, Linley. No talking to the enemy!'

The enemy indeed. What had attracted her? He was a strange-looking fellow: large head, with wavy black hair that was all his own, a terrible pallor, thin unsensual lips. He had made a life in the political marketplace with an unexceptional stall of xenophobic and punitive opinions. Vernon's explanation had always been simple: high-ranking bastard, hot in the sack. But she could have found that anywhere. There must also have been the hidden talent that had got him to where he was and even now was driving him to challenge the PM for his job.

The aide delivered Clive into a horseshoe grouped around Garmony who appeared to be making a speech or telling a story. He broke off to slip his hand into Clive's and murmur intensely, as though they were alone, 'I've been wanting to meet you for years.'

'How do you do.'

Garmony spoke up for the benefit of the company, two of whom were young men with the pleasant, openly dishonest look of diary-page people. The minister was performing and Clive was a kind of prop. 'My wife knows a few of your piano pieces by heart.'

Again. Clive wondered. Was he as domesticated and tame a talent as some of his younger critics claimed, the thinking man's Gorecki?

'She must be good,' he said.

It had been a while since he had met a politician close-up, and what he had forgotten was the eye movements, the restless patrol for new listeners or defectors, or the proximity of some figure of higher status, or some other main chance that might slip by.

Garmony was looking around now, securing his audience. 'She was brilliant. Goldsmith's, then the Guildhall. A fabulous career ahead of her ...' He paused for comic effect. 'Then she met me and chose medicine.'

Only the aide and another staffer, a woman, tittered. The journalists were unmoved. Perhaps they had heard it all before.

The Foreign Secretary's eyes had settled back on Clive. 'There was another thing. I wanted to congratulate you on your commission. The Millennial Symphony. D'you know, that decision went right up to Cabinet level?'

'So I heard. And you voted for me.'

Clive had allowed himself a note of weariness, but Garmony reacted as though he had been effusively thanked. 'Well, it was the least I could do. Some of my colleagues wanted this pop star chap, the ex-Beatle. Anyway, how is it coming along. Almost done?'

'Almost.'

His extremities had been numb for half an hour, but it was only now that the chill finally enveloped his core. In the warmth of his studio he would be in shirtsleeves, working on the final pages of this symphony whose première was only weeks away. He had already missed two deadlines and he longed to be home.

He put out his hand to Garmony. 'It was very nice to meet you. I have to be getting along.'

But the Minister did not take his hand, and was

speaking over him, for there was still a little more to be wrung from the famous composer's presence.

'Do you know, I've often thought that it's the freedom of artists like yourself to pursue your work that makes my own job worthwhile . . .'

More followed in similar style as Clive gazed on, no sign of his growing distaste showing in his expression. Garmony, too, was his generation. High office had eroded his ability to talk levelly with a stranger. Perhaps that was what he offered her in bed, the thrill of the impersonal. A man twitching in front of mirrors. But surely she preferred emotional warmth. Lie still, look at me, really *look* at me. Perhaps it was nothing more than a mistake, Molly and Garmony. Either way, Clive now found it unbearable.

The Foreign Secretary reached his conclusion 'These are the traditions that make us what we are.'

'I was wondering,' Clive said to Molly's ex-lover, 'whether you're still in favour of hanging.'

Garmony was well able to deal with this sudden shift, but his eyes had hardened.

'I think most people are aware of my own position on that. Meanwhile I'm happy to accept the view of Parliament and the collective responsibility of the Cabinet.' He had squared up, and he was also turning on the charm.

The two journalists edged a little closer with their notebooks.

'I see you once said in a speech that Nelson Mandela deserved to be hanged.'

Garmony, who was due to visit South Africa the following month, smiled calmly. The speech had recently been dug up, rather scurrilously, by Vernon's paper. 'I don't think you can reasonably nail people to things they said as hot-head undergraduates.' He paused to chuckle. 'Almost thirty years ago. I bet you said or thought some pretty shocking things yourself.'

'I certainly did,' Clive said. 'Which is my point. If you'd had your way then, there wouldn't be much chance for second thoughts now.'

Garmony inclined his head briefly in acknowledgement. 'Fair enough point. But in the real world, Mr Linley, no justice system can ever be free of human error.'

Then the Foreign Secretary did an extraordinary thing which quite destroyed Clive's theory about the effects of public office and which, in retrospect, he was forced to admire. Garmony reached out and, with his forefinger and thumb, caught hold of the lapel of Clive's overcoat and, drawing him close, spoke in a voice that no one else could hear.

'The very last time I saw Molly she told me you were impotent and always had been.'

'Complete nonsense. She never said that.'

'Of course you're bound to deny it. Thing is, we could discuss it out loud in front of the gentlemen over there, or you could get off my case and make a pleasant farewell. That is to say, fuck off.'

The delivery was rapid and urgent, and as soon as it was over Garmony leaned back, beaming as he pumped the composer's hand, and called out to the aide, 'Mr Linley has kindly accepted an invitation to dinner.' This last may have been an agreed code, for the young man stepped across promptly to usher Clive away while Garmony turned his back on him to say to the journalists, 'A great man, Clive Linley. To air differences and remain friends, the essence of civilised existence, don't you think?'

ii

An hour later Vernon's car, which was absurdly small to have a chauffeur, dropped Clive in South Kensington. Vernon got out to say goodbye.

'Terrible funeral.'

'Not even a drink.'

'Poor Molly.'

Clive let himself into the house and stood in the hallway, absorbing the warmth of the radiators and the silence. A note from his housekeeper told him there was a flask of coffee in the studio. Still in his coat, he walked up there now, took a pencil and a sheet of manuscript paper and, leaning against the grand piano, scribbled down the ten descending notes. He stood by the window, staring at the page, imagining the contrapuntal cellos. There were many days when the commission to write a symphony for the millennium was a ridiculous affliction: a bureaucratic intrusion on his creative independence; the confusion about where exactly Giulio Bo, the great Italian conductor, would be able to rehearse the British Symphony Orchestra; the mild but constant irritation of overexcited or hostile press scrutiny; the fact that he had failed to meet two deadlines – the millennium itself was still years away. There were also days like this one, when he thought of nothing but the music itself and could not stay away.

Keeping his left hand, which was still numb from cold, in the pocket of his coat, he sat at the piano and played the passage as he had written it, slow, chromatic and rhythmically tricksy. There were two time signatures in fact. Then, still with his right hand and at half speed, he improvised the cellos' rising line, and played it again several times, with variations, until he was satisfied. He scribbled out the new part, which was at the very top of the cellos' range, and would sound like some furious energy restrained. Releasing it later, in this final section of the symphony, would be a joy.

He left the piano and poured some coffee which he drank at his usual place by the window. Three thirty, and already dark enough to turn on lights. Molly was ashes. He would work through the night and sleep until lunch. There wasn't really much else to do. Make something, and die. After the coffee he recrossed the room and remained standing, stooped over the keyboard in his overcoat, while he played with both hands by the exhausted afternoon light the notes as he had written them. Almost right, almost the truth. They suggested a dry yearning for something out of reach. Someone. It was at times like this when he used to phone and ask her over, when he was too restless to sit at the piano for long and too excited by new ideas to leave it alone. If she was free she would come over and make tea, or mix exotic drinks, and sit in that worn-out old armchair in the corner. Either they talked, or she made her requests, and listened with eyes closed. Her tastes were surprisingly austere for such a party-loving sort. Bach, Stravinsky, very occasionally Mozart. But she was no longer a girl by then, no longer his lover. They were companionable, too wry with each other to be passionate, and they liked to be free to talk about their own affairs. She was like a sister, judging his women with far more generosity than he ever allowed her men. Otherwise they talked music or food. Now she was fine ash in an alabaster urn for George to keep on top of his wardrobe.

At last he was warm enough, though his left hand still tingled. He removed his coat and slung it over Molly's chair. Before returning to the piano he went about the room turning on lamps. For over two hours he tinkered with the cello part and sketched in further orchestration, oblivious to the darkness outside and the muted, discordant pedal notes of the evening rush hour. It was only a bridging passage to the finale; what fascinated him was the promise, the aspiration – he imagined it as a set of ancient worn steps turning gently out of sight – the yearning to climb on and up, and finally arrive, by way of an expansive shift, at a remote key and, with wisps of sound falling away like so much dissolving mist, at a concluding melody, a valediction, a recognisable melody of piercing beauty that would transcend its unfashionability and seem both to mourn the passing century and all its senseless cruelty, and to celebrate its brilliant inventiveness. Long after the excitement of the first performance was over, long after the millennial celebrations, the fireworks and analyses and potted histories were done with, this irresistible melody would remain as the dead century's elegy.

This was not only Clive's fantasy, it was also that of the

commissioning committee which had chosen a composer who characteristically conceived of, say, this rising passage in terms of steps that were ancient and made of stone. Even his supporters, at least in the '70s, granted the term 'arch-conservative', while his critics preferred 'throwback', but all agreed that along with Schubert and McCartney, Linley could write a melody. The work had been commissioned early so that it could 'play itself' into public consciousness; for example, it had been suggested to Clive that a noisy, urgent brass passage might be used as a signature for the main evening television news. The committee, dismissed by the music establishment as middle-brow, above all longed for a symphony from which could be distilled at least one tune, a hymn, an elegy for the maligned and departed century that could be incorporated into the official proceedings, much as 'Nessun dorma' had been into a football tournament. Incorporated, then set free to take its chances of an independent life in the public mind during the third millennium.

For Clive Linley the matter was simple. He regarded himself as Vaughan Williams' heir, and considered terms like 'conservative' irrelevant, a mistaken borrowing from the political vocabulary. Besides, during the '70s when he was starting to be noticed, atonal and aleatoric music, tone rows, electronics, the disintegration of pitch into sound, in fact the whole modernist project, had become an orthodoxy taught in the colleges. Surely its advocates, rather than he himself, were the reactionaries. In nineteen seventy-five he published a hundred-page book which, like all good manifestos, was both attack and apologia. The old guard of modernism had imprisoned music in the academy where it was jealously professionalised, isolated and rendered sterile, its vital covenant with a general public arrogantly broken. Clive gave a sardonic account of a publicly subsidised 'concert' in a near-deserted church hall, in which the legs of a piano were repeatedly struck with the broken neck of a violin for over an hour. An accompanying programme note explained, with references to the Holocaust, why at this stage in European history no other forms of music were viable. In the small minds of the zealots, Clive insisted, any form of success, however limited, any public appreciation whatsoever, was a sure sign of aesthetic compromise and failure. When the definitive histories of twentieth-century music in the west came to be written, the triumphs would be seen to belong to blues, jazz, rock and the continually evolving traditions of folk music. These forms amply demonstrated that melody, harmony and rhythm were not incompatible with innovation. In art music, only the first half of the century would figure significantly and then only certain composers, among whom Clive did not number the later Schoenberg and 'his like'.

So much for the attack. The apologia borrowed and distorted the well-worn device from Ecclesiastes: it was time to recapture music from the commissars, and it was time to reassert music's essential communicativeness, for it was forged, in Europe, in a humanistic tradition which had always acknowledged the enigma of human nature; it was time to accept that a public performance was a 'secular communion' and it was time to recognise the primacy of rhythm and pitch and the elemental nature of melody. For this to happen without merely repeating the music of the past, we had to evolve a contemporary definition of beauty, and this in turn was not possible without grasping a 'fundamental truth'. At this point Clive boldly borrowed from some unpublished and highly speculative essays by a colleague of Noam Chomsky's, which he had read while on holiday in the man's house on Cape Cod: our capacity to 'read' rhythms, melodies and pleasing harmonies, like our uniquely human ability to learn language, was genetically prescribed. These three elements were found by anthropologists to exist in all musical cultures. Our ear for harmony was hard-wired. (Furthermore, without a surrounding context of harmony, disharmony was meaningless and uninteresting.) Understanding a line of melody was a complex mental act, but it was one which even an infant could perform; we were born into an inheritance, we were *Homo musicus*; defining beauty in music must therefore entail a definition of human nature, which brought us back to the humanities and communicativeness . . .

Clive Linley's *Recalling Beauty* was published to coincide with the première at the Wigmore Hall of his *Symphonic Dervishes for Virtuoso Strings*, a work of such cascading polyphonic brilliance, and interrupted by such a hypnotic lament, that it was loathed and loved in equal measure, thereby securing his reputation and the currency of his book.

Creation apart, the writing of a symphony is physically arduous. Every second of playing time involved writing out, note by note, the parts of up to two dozen instruments, playing them back, making adjustments to the score, playing again, rewriting, then sitting in silence, listening to the inner ear synthesize and orchestrate the vertical array of scribbles and deletions; amending again until the bar is right, and playing it once more on the piano. By midnight Clive had extended and written out in full the rising passage, and was starting on the great orchestral hiatus that would precede the sprawling change of key. By four o'clock in the morning he had written out the major parts and knew exactly how the modulation would work, how the mists would evaporate.

He stood up from the piano, exhausted, satisfied with the progress he had made, but apprehensive: he had brought this massive engine of sound to a point where the real work on the finale could begin, and it could only do so now with an inspired invention – the final melody, in its first and simplest form, baldly stated on a solo wind instrument, or perhaps the first violins. He had reached the core, and felt burdened. He turned out the lamps and walked down to his bedroom. He had no preliminary sketch of an idea, not a scrap, not even a hunch, and he would not find it by sitting at the piano and frowning hard. It could only come in its own time. He knew from experience that the best he could do was relax, step back, while remaining alert and receptive. He would have to take a long walk in the country, or even a series of long walks. He needed mountains, big skies. The Lake District, perhaps. The best ideas caught him by surprise at the end of twenty miles when his mind was elsewhere.

In bed at last, lying on his back in total darkness, taut, resonating from mental effort, he saw jagged rods of primary colour streak across his retina, then fold and writhe into sunbursts. His feet were icy, his arms and chest were hot. Anxieties about work transmuted into the baser metal of simple night fear: illness and death, abstractions which soon found their focus in the sensation he still felt in his left hand. It was cold and inflexible and prickly, as though he had been sitting on it for half an hour. He massaged it with his right hand, and nursed it against the warmth of his stomach. Wasn't this the kind of sensation Molly had when she went to hail that cab by the Dorchester? He had no mate, no wife, no George, to care for him, and perhaps that was a mercy. But what instead? He rolled onto his side and drew the blankets around him. The nursing home, the TV in the day room, bingo, and the old men with their fags and piss and dribbling. He wouldn't stand for it. He would see a doctor in the morning. But that's what Molly did, and they sent her off for tests. They could manage your descent, but they couldn't prevent it. Stay away then, monitor your own decline, then when it was no longer possible to work, or live with dignity, finish it yourself. But how could he stop himself passing that point, the one Molly reached so quickly, when he would be too helpless, too disoriented, too stupid to kill himself?

Ridiculous thoughts! He sat up and groped for the bedside light and pulled out from under a magazine the sleeping pills he preferred to avoid. He took one and leaned back against the pillows, chewing it slowly. Still massaging his hand, he mothered himself with sensible thoughts. His hand had been in the cold, that was all, and he was overtired. His proper business in life was to work, to finish a symphony by finding its lyrical summit. What had oppressed him an hour before was now his solace, and after ten minutes he put out the light and turned on his side: there was always work. He would walk in the Lake District. The magical names were soothing him: Blea Rigg, High Stile, Pavey Ark, Swirl How. He would walk the Langstrath Valley, cross the stream and climb towards Scafell Pike and come home by way of Allen Crags. He knew the circuit well. Striding out, high on the ridge, he would be restored, he would see clearly.

He had swallowed his hemlock, and there'd be no more tormenting fantasies now. This thought too was comfort, so that long before the chemicals had reached his brain, he had drawn his knees towards his chest, and was released. Hard Knott, Ill Bell, Cold Pike, Poor Crag, Poor Molly . . .

II

i

The thought recurred to Vernon Halliday, during an uncharacteristic lull in his morning, that he might not exist. For thirty uninterrupted seconds, he had been sitting at his desk gently palpating his head with his fingertips, and worrying. Since arriving at *The Judge* two hours earlier he had spoken, separately and intensely, to forty people. And not only spoken: in all but two of these exchanges he had decided, prioritised, delegated, chosen, or offered an opinion that was bound to be interpreted as a command. This exercise of authority did not sharpen his sense of self, as it usually did; instead it seemed to Vernon that he was infinitely diluted; he was simply the sum of all the people who had listened to him, and when he was alone, he was nothing at all. When he reached, in solitude, for a thought, there was no one there to think it. His chair was empty; he was finely dissolved throughout the building, from the City Desk on the sixth floor where he was about to intervene to prevent the sacking of a long-serving sub who could not spell, to the basement where parking allocation had brought senior staff to open war and an assistant editor to the brink of resignation. Vernon's chair was empty because he was in Jerusalem, the House of Commons, Cape Town and Manila, globally disseminated like dust; he was on TV and radio, at dinner with some bishops, giving a speech to the oil industry, or a seminar to European Union specialists. In the brief moments during the day when he was alone, a light went out. Even the ensuing darkness encompassed or inconvenienced no one in particular. He could not say for sure that the absence was his.

This sense of absence had been growing since Molly's funeral. It was wearing into him. Last night he had woken beside his sleeping wife and had to touch his own face to be assured he remained a physical entity.

Had Vernon taken a few of his senior staff aside in the canteen and confided about his condition, he might have been alarmed by their lack of surprise. He was widely known as a man without edges, without faults or virtues, as a man who did not fully exist. Within his profession Vernon was revered as a nonentity. It was one of the marvels of newspaper lore, difficult to exaggerate and often recounted in City wine bars, the manner in which he had become editor of *The Judge*. Years back, he had been the bland and hard-working lieutenant for two gifted editors in succession and had shown an instinctive talent for making neither friends nor allies. When the Washington correspondent fell ill, Vernon was ordered to stand in for him. In his third month, at a dinner for the German Ambassador, a congressman mistook Vernon for a writer on the *Washington Post* and tipped him off about a presidential indiscretion – a radical hair implant procured at taxpayers' expense. It was generally accepted that 'Pategate' – a story that dominated American domestic politics for almost a week – had been broken by Vernon Halliday of *The Judge*.

Meanwhile, back in London, one gifted editor was falling to another in bloody battles with a meddlesome board of directors. Vernon's return home coincided with a sudden realignment of proprietorial interests. The stage was littered with the severed limbs and torsos of titans cut down to size. Jack Mobey, the board's own placeman, had failed to take the venerable broadsheet far enough down-market. There was no one left but Vernon.

Now he sat at his desk and tentatively massaged his scalp. Lately he had realised he was learning to live with non-existence. He could not mourn for long the passing of something – himself – that he could no longer quite recall. All this was a worry, but it was a worry that was several days old. There was now a physical symptom. It involved the whole of the right side of his head, both skull and brain somehow, a sensation for which there was simply no word. Or, it might have been the sudden interruption of a sensation so constant and familiar that he had not been conscious of it – like a sound one becomes aware of the moment it stops. He knew exactly when it had begun, the night before, as he had stood up from dinner. It was there when he woke in the morning, continuous and indefinable, not cold, or tight, or airy, though somewhere in between. Perhaps the word was *dead*. His right hemisphere had died. He knew so many people who had died that in his present state of dissociation he could begin to contemplate his own end as a commonplace – a flurry of burying or cremating, a welt of grief raised, then subsiding as life swept on. Perhaps he had already died. Or again, and he felt this strongly, perhaps all that was needed was a couple of sharp taps to the side of the head with a medium-sized hammer. He opened his desk drawer. There was a metal ruler left by Mobey, fourth editor in succession to fail to reverse *The Judge*'s declining circulation. Vernon Halliday was trying not to be the fifth. He had raised the ruler several inches above his right ear when there was a knock on his open door and Jean, his secretary, entered and he was obliged to convert the blow into a pensive scratching.

'The schedule. Twenty minutes.' She peeled off a sheet and gave it to him, and left the rest on the conference table as she went out.

He scanned the lists. Under Foreign, Dibben was writing on 'Garmony's Washington triumph'. That would need to be a sceptical piece, or a hostile one. And if it really was a triumph it could stay off the front page. Under the Home list was, at long last, the piece by the science editor on an anti-gravity machine from a university in Wales. It was an attention-grabber and Vernon had pushed for it, half dreaming of a gizmo you strapped to the bottom of your shoes. In fact the thing turned out to weigh four tons, required nine million volts and didn't work. They were running it anyway, at the bottom of the front page. Also under Home was 'Piano quartet' – quadruplets born to a concert pianist. His deputy, along with Features and the whole Home desk were fighting him over this, hiding their fastidiousness behind a pretence of realism. Four wasn't enough these days, they were saying, and no one had ever heard of the mother, who wasn't pretty anyway and didn't want to talk to the press. Vernon had overruled them. Last month's ABC average was seven thousand lower than the month before. Time was running out for *The Judge*. He was still considering whether to run a story about Siamese twins joined at the hip – one had a weak heart so they couldn't be separated – who had secured a job in local government. 'If we're going to save this paper,' Vernon liked to say at the morning editorial conference, 'you're all going to have to get your hands dirty.' Everyone nodded, nobody agreed. As far as the old hands, the 'grammarians', were concerned, *The Judge* would stand or fall by its intellectual probity. They felt safe in this view because no one on the paper, apart from Vernon's predecessors, had ever been sacked.

The first of the section editors and deputies were filing in when Jean waved to him from the door to pick up the phone. It had to be important because she was mouthing a name. George Lane, her lips said.

Vernon turned his back on the room and remembered how he had avoided Lane at the funeral. 'George. A deeply moving occasion. I was going to drop you a . . .'

'Yes yes. Something's come up. I think you should see it.'

'What sort of thing?'

'Photographs.'

'Can you bike them round?'

'Absolutely not, Vernon. This is very very hot. Can't you come now?'

Not all Vernon's contempt for George Lane had to do

with Molly. Lane owned one and a half per cent of *The Judge* and had put money into the relaunch that marked the fall of Jack Mobey and Vernon's elevation. George thought that Vernon was in his debt. Also, George knew nothing about newspapers which was why he thought the editor of a national daily could saunter out of his office to cross the entire width of London to Holland Park at eleven thirty in the morning.

'I'm rather busy at present,' Vernon said.

'I'm doing you a big favour here. Sort of thing the *News of the World* would kill for.'

'I could be there sometime after nine this evening.'

'Very well. I'll see you then,' George said huffily, and rang off.

By now every chair but one at the conference table had been taken, and as Vernon lowered himself into it the conversation subsided. He touched the side of his head. Now that he was in company again, back on the job, his interior absence was no longer an affliction. Yesterday's paper was spread before him. He said into the near silence, 'Who subbed the environment leader?'

'Pat Redpath.'

'On this paper "hopefully" is not a sentence adverb, nor will it ever be, especially in a leader for Godsakes. And none . . .' He trailed away for dramatic effect, while pretending to scan the piece. '"None" usually takes a singular verb. Can we get these two things generally understood?'

Vernon was aware of the approval round the table. This was the kind of thing the grammarians liked to hear.

Together they would see the paper into the grave with its syntax pure.

Crowd-pleaser dispensed, he pressed on at speed. One of his few successful innovations, perhaps his only one so far, was to have reduced the daily conference from forty to fifteen minutes by means of a few modestly imposed rules: no more than five minutes on the post-mortem – what's done is done; no joke telling and, above all, no anecdotes; he didn't tell them, so no one else could. He turned to the international pages and frowned. 'An exhibition of pottery shards in Ankara? A news item? Eight hundred words? I simply don't get it, Frank.'

Frank Dibben, the deputy foreign editor, explained, perhaps with a trace of mockery. 'Well, you see Vernon, it represents a fundamental paradigm shift in our understanding of the influence of the early Persian Empire on . . .'

'Paradigm shifts in broken pots aren't news, Frank.'

Grant McDonald, the deputy editor, who was sitting at Vernon's elbow, cut in gently. 'Thing is, Julie failed to file from Rome. They had to fill the . . .'

'Not again. What is it now?'

'Hepatitis C.'

'So what about AP?'

Dibben spoke up. 'This was more interesting.'

'You're wrong. It's a complete turn-off. Even the *TLS* wouldn't run it.'

They moved on to the day's schedule. In turn the editors summarised the stories on their lists. When it came to

Frank's turn he pushed for his Garmony story to lead the front page.

Vernon heard him out, and then: 'He's in Washington when he should be Brussels. He's cutting a deal with the Americans behind the Germans' backs. Short-term gain, long-term disaster. He was a terrible Home Secretary, he's even worse at the Foreign Office and he'll be the ruin of us if he's ever Prime Minister – which is looking more and more likely.'

'Well yes,' Frank agreed, his softness of tone concealing his fury about the Ankara put-down. 'You said all that in your leader, Vernon. Surely the point is, not whether we agree with the deal, but whether it's significant.'

Vernon was wondering whether he might just bring himself to let Frank go. What was he doing, wearing an earring?

'Quite right, Frank,' Vernon said cordially. 'We're in Europe. The Americans want us in Europe. The special relationship is history. The deal has no significance. The coverage stays on the inside pages. Meanwhile, we'll continue to give Garmony a hard time.'

They listened to the sports editor whose pages Vernon had recently doubled at the expense of arts and books. Then it was the turn of Lettice O'Hara, the features editor.

'I need to know if we can go ahead with the Welsh children's home.'

Vernon said, 'I've seen the guest list. A lot of big cheeses. We can't afford the legal costs if it goes wrong.'

Lettice looked relieved, and began to describe an

investigative piece she had commissioned on a medical scandal in Holland.

'Apparently, there are doctors exploiting the euthanasia laws to . . .'

Vernon interrupted her.

'I want to run the Siamese twins story in Friday's paper.'

There were groans. But who was going to object first? Lettice. 'We don't even have a picture.'

'So send someone to Middlesbrough this afternoon.' There was sullen silence, so Vernon continued. 'Look, they work in a section of the local hygiene department called Forward Planning. It's a sub's dream.'

The home editor, Jeremy Ball, said, 'We spoke last week and it was OK. Then he phoned yesterday. I mean, it was the other half. The other head. Doesn't want to talk. Doesn't want a picture.'

'Oh God!' Vernon cried. 'Don't you see? That's all part of the story. They've fallen out. First thing anyone would want to know – how do they settle disputes?'

Lettice was looking gloomy. She said, 'Apparently there are bite marks. On both faces.'

'Brilliant!' Vernon exclaimed. 'No one else is on to this yet. Friday please. Page three. Now, moving on. Lettice. This eight-page chess supplement. Frankly, I'm not convinced.'

Another three hours passed before Vernon found himself alone again. He was in the washroom, looking in the mirror while rinsing his hands. The image was there, but he wasn't entirely convinced. The sensation, or the non-sensation, still occupied the right side of his head like a tight-fitting cap. When he trailed his finger across his scalp, he could identify the border, the demarcation line where feeling on the left side became not quite its opposite, but its shadow, or its ghost.

His hands were under the drier when Frank Dibben came in. Vernon sensed that the younger man had followed him in to talk, for a lifetime's experience had taught him that a male journalist did not urinate easily, or by preference, in the presence of his editor.

'Look Vernon,' Frank said from where he stood at the urinal. 'I'm sorry about this morning. You're absolutely right about Garmony. I was completely out of order.'

Rather than look round from the drier and be obliged to watch the deputy foreign editor at his business, Vernon gave himself another turn with the hot air. Dibben was in fact relieving himself copiously, thunderously even. Yes, if Vernon ever sacked anyone, it would be Frank, who was shaking himself vigorously, for just a second too long, and pressing on with his apology.

'I mean, you're absolutely right about not giving him too much space.'

Cassius is hungry, Vernon thought. He'll head his department, then he'll want my job.

Dibben turned to the washbasin. Vernon put his hand lightly on his shoulder, the forgiving touch.

'It's all right, Frank. I'd rather hear opposing views at conference. That's the whole point of it.'

'It's kind of you to say that, Vernon. I just wouldn't want you to think I was going soft on Garmony.'

This festival of first-naming marked the end of the exchange. Vernon gave a little reassuring laugh and stepped out into the corridor. Waiting for him right by the door was Jean with a bundle of correspondence for him to sign. Behind her was Jeremy Ball, and behind him was Tony Montano, the managing director. Someone else whom Vernon could not see was just joining the back of the queue. The editor began to move towards his office, signing the letters as he went and listening to Jean's rundown of his week's appointments. Everyone moved with him. Ball was saying, 'This Middlesbrough photo. I'd like to avoid the trouble we got into over the wheelchair Olympics. I thought we'd go for something pretty straightforward . . .'

'I want an exciting picture, Jeremy. I can't see them in the same week, Jean. It wouldn't look right. Tell him Thursday.'

'I had in mind an upright Victorian sort of thing. A dignified portrait.'

'He's leaving for Angola. The idea was he'd go straight out to Heathrow as soon as he'd seen you.'

'Mr Halliday?'

'I don't want dignified portraits, even in obits. Get them to show us how they gave each other the bite marks. OK, I'll see him before he leaves. Tony, is this about the parking?'

'I'm afraid I've seen a draft of his resignation letter.'

'Surely there's one little space we can find.'

'We've tried all that. Head of maintenance is offering to sell his for three thousand pounds.'

'Don't we run the risk of sensationalism?'

'Sign it in two places, and initial where I've marked.'

'It's not a risk, Jeremy. It's a promise. But Tony. Head of maintenance doesn't even have a car.'

'Mr Halliday?'

'The space is his by right.'

'Offer him five hundred. Is that the lot, Jean?'

'I'm not prepared to do that.'

'The letter of thanks to the bishops is just being typed.'

'What if they were both talking on the phone?'

'Excuse me. Mr Halliday?'

'It's too weak. I want a picture that tells a story. Dirty hands time, remember? Look, you'd better throw maintenance out of his space if he's not using it . . .'

'They'll strike, like last time. All the terminals went down.'

'Fine. Your choice, Tony. Five hundred pounds or the terminals.'

'I'll ask someone from the picture desk to pop up and . . .'

'Don't bother. Just send the guy to Middlesbrough.'

'Mr Halliday? Are you Mr Vernon Halliday?'

'Who are you?'

The talking group came to a halt and a thin, balding man in a black suit whose jacket was tightly buttoned pushed his way forward and tapped Vernon on the elbow with an envelope which he put into Vernon's hands. Then the man planted his feet well apart and read in a declamatory monotone from a sheet of paper which he held in front of him with two hands. 'By the power of the above headed Court in the Principal Registry invested in me, I make known to you, Vernon Theobald Halliday, the order of said Court as follows: that Vernon Theobald Halliday of thirteen, The Rooks, London NW1 and editor of *The Judge* newspaper, shall not publish, nor cause to have published, nor distribute or disseminate by electronic or any other means, nor describe in print, or cause such descriptions of the proscribed matter hereafter to be referred to as the material, to be printed, nor describe the nature and terms of this order; the aforesaid material being . . .'

The thin man fumbled the page-turn and the editor, his secretary, the home editor, the deputy foreign editor and the managing director inclined towards the tipstaff, waiting.

'. . . all photographic reproductions, or versions of such reproductions whether engraved, drawn, painted or produced by any other means, of the likeness of Mr John Julian Garmony of number one, Carlton Gardens . . .'

'Garmony!'

Everyone began talking at once and the final rhetorical flourishes of the thin man in the suit two sizes too small were lost. Vernon set off towards his office. These were blanket provisions. But they had nothing on Garmony, nothing at all. He reached his office, kicked the door shut behind him and dialled.

'George. These photographs are of Garmony.'

'I'm saying nothing until you get here.'

'He's already served an injunction.'

'I told you they were hot. I think your public-interest arguments will be irresistible.'

As soon as Vernon hung up his private line rang. It was Clive Linley. Vernon hadn't seen him since the funeral.

'I need to talk to you about something.'

'Clive, this isn't really the best moment for me.'

'No, quite. I need to *see* you. It's important. What about after work tonight?'

There was a heaviness in his old friend's tone that made Vernon reluctant to put him off. All the same, he tried half-heartedly.

'It's rather a hectic day . . .'

'It won't take long. It's important, really important.'

'Well look, I'm seeing George Lane tonight. I suppose I could call in on my way.'

'Vernon, I'm very grateful to you.'

He had a few seconds after the call to wonder about Clive's manner. So pressing in a lugubrious way, and rather formal. Clearly, something terrible had happened, and he began to feel embarrassed by his ungenerous response. Clive was a true friend when Vernon's second marriage came apart, and he encouraged him to go for the editorship when everybody else thought he was wasting his time. Four years ago, when Vernon was laid up with a rare viral infection of the spine, Clive visited almost every day, bringing books, music, videos and champagne. And in 1987, when Vernon was out of a job for several months, Clive had lent him ten thousand pounds. Two years later Vernon discovered by accident that Clive had borrowed the money from his bank. And now, in his friend's moment of need, Vernon was behaving like a swine.

When he tried to call back there was no reply. He was about to dial again when the managing director came in with the newspaper's lawyer.

'You've got something on Garmony you didn't tell us about.'

'Absolutely not, Tony. Obviously, something's floating around and he's panicked. Someone should check if he's served on any of the others.'

The lawyer said, 'We have. He hasn't.'

Tony was looking distrustful. 'And you know nothing?'

'Not a thing. Bolt from the blue.'

There were more suspicious questions of this sort and more denials from Vernon.

As they were leaving Tony said, 'You won't do anything without us now, will you, Vernon?'

'You know me,' he said and winked. As soon as the two had gone he reached for the phone and was just beginning on Clive's number when he heard a commotion in the outer office. His door was kicked open and a woman came running in, followed by Jean who rolled her eyes heaven-wards for the editor's benefit. The woman stood in front of his desk, weeping. In her hand was a crumpled letter. It was the dyslexic sub. It was hard to make sense of everything she was saying, but Vernon could discern one repeated line.

'You said you'd stand by me. You *promised*!'

He could not know it then, but the moment before she entered his room was the last occasion he would be alone until he left the building at nine thirty that evening.

iii

Molly used to say that what she loved most about Clive's house was that he had lived in it so long. In 1970, when most of his contemporaries were still in rented rooms and several years away from buying their first damp basement flats, Clive inherited from a rich and childless uncle a gigantic stuccoed villa with a purpose-built two-storey artist's studio on the third and fourth floors whose vast arched windows faced north over a mess of pitched roofs. In keeping with the times and his youth – he was twenty-one – he had the outside painted purple and filled the inside with his friends, mostly musicians. Certain celebrities passed through. John Lennon and Yoko Ono spent a week there. Jimi Hendrix stayed a night, and was the likely cause of a fire which destroyed the banisters. As the decade progressed, the house calmed down. Friends still stayed over, but only for a night or two, and no one slept on the floor. The stucco was restored to cream, Vernon was a lodger for a year, Molly stayed for a summer, a grand piano was carried up to the studio, bookshelves were built, oriental rugs were laid over worn-out carpets and various pieces of Victorian furniture were carried in. Apart from a few old mattresses, very little was ever carried out, and this must have been what Molly liked, for the house was a history of an adult life, of changing tastes, fading passions and growing wealth. The earliest Woolworth's cutlery was still in the same kitchen drawer as the antique silver set. Oil paintings by English and Danish impressionists hung in proximity to faded posters advertising Clive's early triumphs or famous rock concerts – the Beatles at Shea stadium, Bob Dylan on the Isle of Wight, the Rolling Stones at Altamont. Some of the posters were worth more than the paintings.

By the early 'eighties this was the home of a youngish, wealthy composer – by then he had written the music for Dave Spieler's hit movie, *Christmas on the Moon* – and a certain dignity, so Clive considered in his better moments, seemed to fall from the gloomy high ceilings onto the huge lumpy sofas and all the stuff, not quite junk, not quite antique, that had been bought in Lots Road. The impression of seriousness was furthered when an energetic housekeeper started to keep order. The not-quite junk was dusted or polished and began to look antique. The last of the lodgers departed and the silence in the house was workmanlike. Over several years Clive seemed to race through two childless marriages relatively unscathed. The three women he had known closely lived abroad. The one he was with now, Susie Marcellan, was in New York and when she came over it was never for very long. The years and all the successes had narrowed his life to its higher purpose; he was becoming not quite zealous, but cagey about his privacy. Profile writers and photographers were never invited in these days, and the time had long passed when Clive snatched hours between friends or lovers or parties to write a sudden daring opening, or even a complete song. The open house was no more.

But Vernon still took pleasure in his visits, for he had done a lot of his own growing up here and had only fond memories of girlfriends, hilarious evenings with various drugs, and working through the nights in a small bedroom at the rear of the house. Back in the days of typewriters and carbon copies. Even now, as he left his taxi and mounted the steps to the front door, he experienced again, though only vestigially, a sensation he never had these days, of genuine anticipation, the feeling that anything might happen.

When Clive opened the door Vernon saw no immediate signs of distress or crisis. The two friends embraced in the hall.

'There's champagne in the fridge.'

He fetched the bottle and two glasses, and Vernon followed him up the stairs. The house had a closeted atmosphere and he guessed that Clive had not been out for a day or two. A half-open door revealed the bedroom to be in a mess. He sometimes asked the housekeeper not to come in when he was working hard. The state of the studio confirmed the impression. Manuscript paper covered the floor, dirty plates, cups and wine glasses were strewn around the piano and the keyboard and midi computer on which Clive sometimes worked out his orchestrations. The air felt close and damp as though it had been breathed many times.

'Sorry about the mess.'

Together they cleared books and papers off the arm-chairs, then sat with their champagne and small-talk. Clive told Vernon about his encounter with Garmony at Molly's funeral.

'The Foreign Secretary actually said "fuck off"?' Vernon asked. 'We could have used that in the diary.'

'Quite. I'm trying to keep out of everyone's way.'

Since they were on Garmony, Vernon gave an account of his two conversations that morning with George Lane. It was just the kind of story to appeal to Clive, but he showed no curiosity about the photographs and the injunction and seemed to be only half listening. He was on his feet as soon as the story was over. He refilled their glasses. The silence that announced the change of subject was heavy. Clive set down his glass and went to the far end of the studio, then paced back, gently massaging the palm of his left hand.

'I've been thinking about Molly,' he said at last. 'The way she died, the speed of it, her helplessness, how she wouldn't have wanted it that way. Stuff we've talked about before.'

He paused. Vernon drank and waited.

'Well, the thing is this. I've had my own little scare lately . . .' He raised his voice to forestall Vernon's concern. 'Probably nothing. You know, the sort of thing that gives you the sweats at night, and by daylight seems like stupidity. That's not what I want to talk about. It's almost certainly nothing, but there's nothing lost by what I'm going to ask you. Just supposing I did get ill in a major way, like Molly, and I started to go downhill and make terrible mistakes, you know, errors of judgement, not knowing the names of things or who I was, that kind of thing. I'd like to know there was someone who'd help me to finish it . . . I mean, help me to die. Especially if I got to the point where I couldn't make the decision for myself, or act on it. So, what I'm saying is this – I'm asking you, as my oldest friend, to help me if it ever got to the point where you could see that it was the right thing. Just as we might have helped Molly if we'd been able . . .'

Clive trailed away, a little disconcerted by Vernon who stared at him with his glass raised, as though frozen in the act of drinking. Clive cleared his throat noisily.

'It's an odd thing to ask, I know. It's also illegal in this country and I wouldn't want you to put yourself on the wrong side of the law, assuming, of course, you were to say yes. But there are ways, and there are places and if it came to it, I'd want you to get me there on a plane. It's a heavy responsibility, something I could only ask of a close friend like yourself. All I can say is that I'm not in a state of panic or anything. I have given it a lot of thought.'

Then, because Vernon still sat in silence, staring, he added with some embarrassment, 'Well, there it is.'

Vernon set down his glass and scratched his head, and then stood.

'You don't want to talk about this scare you've had?'

'Absolutely not.'

Vernon glanced at his watch. He was late for George. He said, 'Well look, it's quite a thing you're asking me. It needs some thought.'

Clive nodded. Vernon moved towards the door and led

49

the way down the stairs. In the hallway they embraced again. Clive opened the door and Vernon stepped out into the night.

'I'll need to think about it.'

'Quite so. Thanks for coming.'

Both men accepted that the nature of the request, its intimacy and self-conscious reflection on their friendship, had created, for the moment, an uncomfortable emotional proximity which was best dealt with by their parting without another word, Vernon walking quickly up the street in search of a taxi, and Clive going back up the stairs, to his piano.

iv

Lane himself opened the door of his Holland Park mansion.

'You're late.'

Vernon, who assumed that George was trying on the part of press lord summoning his editor, declined to apologise or even reply, and followed his host across a bright hallway into the living room. Fortunately, there was nothing here to remind Vernon of Molly. The room was furnished in what he had once heard her describe as the Buckingham Palace style; thick mustard-yellow carpets, big dusty-pink sofas and armchairs with raised patterns of vines and scrolls, brown oil paintings of racehorses at grass, and reproduction Fragonards of bucolic ladies on swings in immense gilt frames, and the whole opulent emptiness overlit by lacquered brass lamps. George reached the massive brecciated marble surround of the coal-effect gas fire, and turned.

'You'll take a glass of port?'

Vernon realised that he had had nothing to eat since a cheese and lettuce sandwich at lunchtime. Why else would George's pretentious construction have made him feel so irritable? And what was George doing wearing a silk dressing-gown over his day clothes? The man was simply preposterous.

'Thanks. I will.'

They sat almost twenty feet apart, with the hissing fireplace between them. Had he been alone for half a minute, Vernon thought, he might have crawled over to the fender and knocked the right side of his head on it. Even in company now, he did not feel right.

'I've seen the ABC figures,' George said gravely. 'Not good.'

'The rate of decline is slowing,' was Vernon's automatic response, his mantra.

'But it's still a decline.'

'These things take time to turn around.' Vernon tasted his port and protected himself with the recollection that George owned a mere one and a half per cent of *The Judge* and knew nothing about the business. It was also useful to remember that his fortune, his publishing 'empire', was rooted in an energetic exploitation of the weak-headed: hidden numerical codes in the Bible foretold the future, the Incas hailed from outer space, the Holy Grail, the Ark of the Covenant, the Second Coming, the Third Eye, the Seventh Seal, Hitler was alive and well in Peru. It was not easy to be lectured by George on the ways of the world.

'It seems to me,' he was saying, 'that what you need now is one big story, something that'll catch fire, something your opponents will have to run with just to keep up.'

What was needed for the circulation to stop going down was for the circulation to go up. But Vernon kept a neutral expression, for he knew that George was working his way round to the photographs.

Vernon tried to speed him up. 'We've got a good story

on Friday about a pair of Siamese twins in local government . . .'

'Pah!'

It worked. George was suddenly on his feet.

'That's not a story, Vernon. That's tittle-tattle. I'll show you a story. I'll show you why Julian Garmony is running round the Inns of Court with his thumb up his arse! Come with me.'

They went back down the hall, past the kitchen and along a narrower corridor that ended in a door which George opened with a Yale key. Part of the complicated arrangement of his marriage had been that Molly kept herself, her guests, and her stuff separate in a wing of the house. She was spared the sight of her old friends stifling their amusement at George's pomposity, and he escaped the tidal waves of Molly's disorder engulfing the rooms of the house used for entertaining. Vernon had visited Molly's apartment many times, but he always used the external entrance. Now, as George pushed the door open, Vernon tensed. He felt unprepared. He would have preferred to look at the photographs in George's part of the house.

In the semi-darkness, during the seconds it took George to fumble for the light switch, Vernon experienced for the first time the proper impact of Molly's death – the plain fact of her absence. The recognition was brought on by familiar smells that he had already started to forget – her perfume, her cigarettes, the dried flowers she kept in the bedroom, coffee beans, the bakery warmth of laundered clothes. He had talked about her at length, and he had thought of her too, but only in snatches during his crowded working days, or while drifting into sleep, and until now he had never really missed her in his heart, or felt the insult of knowing he would never see or hear her again. She was his friend, perhaps the best he had ever had, and she had gone. He could easily have made a fool of himself in front of George whose outline was blurring even now. This particular kind of desolation, a painful constriction right behind his face, above the roof of his mouth, he hadn't known since childhood, since prep school. Homesick for Molly. He concealed a gasp of self-pity behind a loud adult cough.

The place was exactly as she had left it, the day she finally consented to move to a bedroom in the main house to be imprisoned and nursed by George. As they passed the bathroom, Vernon glimpsed a skirt of hers he remembered, draped over the towel rail, and a towel and a bra lying on the floor. Over a quarter of a century ago she and Vernon had made a household for almost a year, in a tiny rooftop flat on the Rue de Seine. There were always damp towels on the floor then, and cataracts of her underwear tumbling from the drawers she never closed, a big ironing board that was never folded away, and in the one over-filled wardrobe, dresses, crushed and shouldering sideways like commuters on the Métro. Magazines, make-up, bank statements, bead necklaces, flowers, knickers, ashtrays, invitations, tampons, LPs, airplane tickets, high-heeled shoes – there was not a single surface left uncovered by something of Molly's, so that when Vernon was meant to be working at home, he took to writing in a café along the street. And yet each morning she arose fresh from the shell of this girly squalor, like a Botticelli Venus, to present herself, not naked of course, but sleekly groomed, at the offices of Paris *Vogue*.

'In here,' George said, and led the way into the living room. There was a large brown envelope on a chair. As George was reaching for it, Vernon had time to glance around. She could walk in at any moment. There was a book on Italian gardens lying face down on the floor and, on a low table, three wine glasses, each with a lining of greyish-green mould. Perhaps he himself had been drinking from one. He tried to remember his last visit here, but the occasions blurred. There were long conversations about her move to the main house which she dreaded and resisted, knowing it would be a one-way journey. The alternative was a nursing home. Vernon and all her other friends advised her to stay in Holland Park, believing familiarity would serve her better. How wrong they were. She would have been freer, even under the strictest institutional regime, than she turned out to be in George's care.

He was gesturing Vernon into a chair, and relishing the moment as he pulled the photographs from the envelope. Vernon was still thinking of Molly. Were there moments of clarity as she slid under, when she felt abandoned by the friends who did not come to visit her, not knowing they were barred by George? If she cursed her friends, she surely would have cursed Vernon.

George had placed the photographs – three ten by eights – face down on his lap. He was enjoying what he took by

Vernon's silence to be speechless impatience. He piled on the supposed agony by talking with slow deliberation.

'I should say one thing first. I've no idea why she took these, but one thing is sure. It could only have been done with Garmony's consent. He's looking straight at the lens. The copyright was hers and, as the sole trustee of her estate, I effectively own it. It goes without saying, I shall expect *The Judge* to protect its sources.'

He peeled one off and passed it across. For a moment it made no sense, beyond its glossy blacks and whites, then it resolved into a medium close-up. Incredible. Vernon stretched out his hand for another; head to foot and tightly cropped; and then the third, three-quarter profile. He turned back to the first, all other thoughts suddenly dispelled. Then he studied the second and third again, seeing them fully now and feeling waves of distinct responses: astonishment first, followed by a wild inward hilarity. Suppressing it gave him a sense of levitating from his chair. Next, he experienced ponderous responsibility – or was it power? A man's life, or at least his career, was in his hands. And who could tell, perhaps Vernon was in a position to change the country's future for the better. And his paper's circulation.

'George,' he said at last. 'I need to think about this very carefully.'

v

Half an hour later Vernon left George's house with the envelope in his hands. He stopped a cab and, having asked the driver to start his clock and stay put by the side of the road, he sat in the back for a few minutes, soothed by the engine's throb, massaging the right side of his head, and considering what to do. Finally, he asked for South Kensington.

The light was on in the studio, but Vernon did not ring the bell. At the top of the steps he scribbled a note which he thought the housekeeper was likely to read first and which he therefore kept vague. He folded it over twice before pushing it through the front door and hurrying back to the waiting taxi. *Yes, on one condition only: that you'd do the same for me. V.*

III

III

i

As Clive had predicted, the melody was elusive as long as he remained in London, in his studio. Each day he made attempts, little sketches, bold stabs, but he produced nothing but quotations, thinly or well disguised, of his own work. Nothing sprang free in its own idiom, with its own authority, to offer the element of surprise that would be the guarantee of originality. Each day, after abandoning the attempt, he committed himself to easier, duller tasks, like fleshing out orchestrations, rewriting messy pages of manuscript and elaborating on a sliding resolution of minor chords that marked the opening of the slow movement. Three appointments evenly spread over eight days kept him from leaving for the Lake District: he had said months before that he would attend a fund-raising dinner; as a favour to a nephew who worked in radio, he had agreed to give a five-minute talk, and he had let himself be persuaded into judging a composition prize at a local school. Finally, he had to delay by yet another day because Vernon asked to meet him.

During this time, when he wasn't working, Clive studied his maps, rubbed liquid wax into his walking boots and checked his equipment – important when planning a winter walk in the mountains. It would have been possible to back out of his engagements by assuming the licence of the free artistic spirit, but he loathed such arrogance. He had a number of friends who played the genius card when it suited, failing to show up to this or that in the belief that whatever local upset it caused, it could only increase respect for the compelling nature of their high calling. These types – novelists were by far the worst – managed to convince friends and families that not only their working hours, but every nap and stroll, every fit of silence, depression or drunkenness bore the exculpatory ticket of high intent. A mask for mediocrity, was Clive's view. He didn't doubt that the calling was high, but bad behaviour was not a part of it. Perhaps every century there was an exception or two to be made; Beethoven, yes; Dylan Thomas, *most certainly not.*

He told no one he was stalled in his work. Instead, he said he was off on a short walking holiday. In fact, he didn't regard himself as blocked at all. Sometimes the work was hard and you had to do whatever experience had taught you was most effective. So he stayed on in London, attended the dinner, gave the talk, judged the prize and, for the first time in his life, had a major disagreement with Vernon. It was not until the first day of March that he arrived at Euston station and found an empty first-class compartment on a train bound for Penrith.

He enjoyed long train journeys for the soothing rhythm they gave to thought – exactly what he needed after his confrontation with Vernon. But settling down in the compartment was not as easy as it should have been. Coming along the platform, in a dark mood, he had become aware of an unevenness in his stride, as though one leg had grown longer than the other. Once he had found his seat he removed his shoe and discovered a flattened black mass of chewing gum embedded deep in the zig-zag tread of the sole. Upper lip arched in disgust, he was still picking, cutting and scraping away with a pocket knife as the train began to move. Beneath the patina of grime, the gum was still slightly pink, like flesh, and the smell of peppermint was faint but distinct. How appalling, the intimate contact with the contents of a stranger's mouth, the bottomless vulgarity of people who chewed gum and who let it fall from their lips where they stood. He returned from washing his hands, spent some minutes searching in desperation for his reading glasses before finding them on the seat beside him, and then realised he had not brought a pen. When at last he directed his attention out of the window, a familiar misanthropy had settled on him and he saw in the built landscape sliding by nothing but ugliness and pointless activity.

In his corner of west London, and in his self-preoccupied daily round, it was easy for Clive to think of civilisation as the sum of all the arts, along with design, cuisine, good wine and the like. But now it appeared that this was what it really was – square miles of meagre modern houses whose principal purpose was the support of TV aerials and dishes; factories producing worthless junk to be advertised on the televisions and, in dismal lots, lorries queuing to distribute it; and everywhere else, roads and the tyranny of traffic. It looked like a raucous dinner party the morning after. No one would have wished it this way, but no one had been asked. Nobody planned it, nobody wanted it, but most people had to live in it. To watch it mile after mile, who would have guessed that kindness or the imagination, that Purcell or Britten, Shakespeare or Milton, had ever existed? Occasionally, as the train gathered speed and they swung further away from London, countryside appeared and with it the beginnings of beauty, or the memory of it, until seconds later it dissolved into a river straightened to a concreted sluice or a sudden agricultural wilderness without hedges or trees, and roads, new roads probing endlessly, shamelessly, as though all that mattered was to be elsewhere. As far as the welfare of every other living form on earth was concerned, the human project was not just a failure, it was a mistake from the very beginning.

If anyone was to blame it was Vernon. Clive had travelled this line often in the past and had never felt bleak about the view. He couldn't put it down to chewing gum, or a mislaid pen. Their row of the evening before was still sounding in his ears, and he worried that the echoes would pursue him into the mountains and destroy his peace. And it was hardly just a clash of voices he still carried with him, it was growing dismay at his friend's behaviour, and a gathering sense that he had never really known Vernon at all. He turned away from the window. To think, only the week before he had made a most unusual and intimate request of his friend. What a mistake that was, especially now that the sensation in his left hand had vanished completely. Just a foolish anxiety brought on by Molly's funeral. One of those occasional bouts of fearing death. But how vulnerable he had made himself that night. It was no comfort that Vernon had asked the same for himself; all it cost him was a scribbled note pushed through the door. And perhaps that was typical of a certain . . . imbalance in their friendship that had always been there and which Clive had been aware of somewhere in his heart and had always pushed away, disliking himself for unworthy thoughts. Until now. Yes, a certain lopsidedness in their friendship which, if he cared to consider, made last night's confrontation less surprising.

There was the time, for example, way back, when Vernon stayed for a year and never once offered to pay rent. And was it not generally true that over the years it had been Clive rather than Vernon who had provided the music – in every sense? The wine, the food, the house, the musicians and other interesting company, the initiatives that brought Vernon to rented houses with lively friends in Scotland, the mountains of northern Greece, and on the shores of Long Island. When had Vernon ever proposed and arranged some fascinating pleasure? When was Clive last a guest in Vernon's house? Three or four years ago perhaps. Why had he never properly acknowledged the act of friendship that lay behind his borrowing a large sum to see Vernon through a difficult time? When he had an infection of the spine, Clive visited almost every day; when Clive slipped on the pavement outside his house and broke his ankle, Vernon sent his secretary round with a bag of books from *The Judge*'s books page slush pile.

Put most crudely, what did he, Clive, really derive from this friendship? He had given, but what had he ever received? What bound them? They had Molly in common, there were the accumulated years and the habits of friendship, but there was really nothing at its centre, nothing for Clive. A generous explanation for the imbalance might have evoked Vernon's passivity and self-absorption. Now, after last night, Clive was inclined to see these as merely elements of a larger fact – Vernon's lack of principle.

Outside the compartment window, unseen by Clive, a deciduous woodland slid by, its winter geometry silvered by unmelted frost. Further on, a slow river eased through brown fringes of sedge and, beyond the flood plain, icy pastures were laced with dry-stone walls. On the edges of a rusty-looking town, an expanse of industrial wasteland was being returned to forest; saplings in plastic tubes stretched almost to the horizon where bulldozers were spreading topsoil. But Clive stared ahead at the empty seat opposite, lost to the self-punishing convolutions of his fervent social accounting, unknowingly bending and colouring the past through the prism of his unhappiness. Other thoughts diverted him occasionally, and for periods he read, but this was the theme of his northward journey, the long and studied redefinition of a friendship.

In Penrith some hours later, it was a great relief to step away from this brooding and go along the platform with his bags in search of a taxi. It was over twenty miles to Stonethwaite and he was happy to lose himself in small-talk with the driver. Because it was midweek and out of season, Clive was the hotel's only guest. He had asked for the room he had taken three or four times before, the only one with a table to work at. Despite the cold he opened the window wide so he could breathe the distinctive winter Lakeland air while he unpacked – peaty water, wet rock, mossy earth. He ate alone in the bar under the gaze of a stuffed fox mounted in a glass case, frozen in a predatory crouch. After a short walk in total darkness round the edges of the hotel car park, he came back indoors, said goodnight to his waitress and returned to his tiny room. After reading for an hour he lay in darkness, listening to the swollen crashing beck, knowing that his subject was bound to return and that it would be better to indulge it now than take it with him on his walk the next day. It wasn't the disillusionment that forced itself on him now. There were his memories of the conversation, and then something beyond; what had been said, and then what he would like to have said to Vernon now that he had had hours to reflect. It was remembering, and it was also fantasising: he imagined a drama in which he gave himself all the best lines, resonant lines of sad reasonableness whose indictments were all the more severe and unanswerable for their compression and emotional restraint.

What actually happened was this: Vernon phoned in the late morning, using words so close to those Clive had spoken the week before that they seemed like conscious quotation, a playful calling in of a debt. Vernon had to talk to him, it was very pressing, the phone wouldn't do, he had to *see* him, it had to be today.

Clive hesitated. He had intended to catch the afternoon train to Penrith, but he said, 'Well, come round and I'll make supper.'

He rearranged his travel plans, brought up two good burgundies from the cellar, and cooked. Vernon arrived an hour late and Clive's first impression was that his friend had lost weight. His face was long and thin and unshaved, his overcoat looked many sizes too large, and when he set down his briefcase to accept a glass of wine his hand was trembling.

He downed the Chambertin Clos de Bèze like a lager and said, 'What a week, what a terrible week.' He held out his glass for a refill, and Clive, relieved that he had not started with the Richebourg, obliged.

'We were in court three hours this morning and we won. You'd think that would be the end of it. But the whole staff's against me, almost all of them. The building's in uproar. It's a marvel we got a paper out tonight. There's a chapel meeting going on now and they're certain to pass a motion of no confidence in me. Management and the board are standing firm, so that's fine. It's a fight to the death.'

Clive gestured towards a chair and Vernon flopped into it, put his elbows on the kitchen table, covered his face with his hands and wailed, 'These prissy bastards. I'm trying to save their arse-wipe newspaper and their piss-pot jobs. They'd rather lose everything than dangle a single fucking modifier. They don't live in the real world. They deserve to starve.' Clive had no idea what Vernon was talking about, but he said nothing. Vernon's glass was empty again, so Clive filled it and turned away to lift two poussins from the oven. Vernon heaved his briefcase onto his lap. Before opening it he took a deep, calming breath and another slug of the Chambertin. He sprung the catches, hesitated, and spoke in a lower voice.

'Look, I'd like your view on this, not just because you've got a personal connection and you already know a little about it. It's because you're not in the business and I need an outsider's view. I think I'm going mad . . .'

This last he was murmuring to himself as he delved into the case and produced a large cardboard-backed envelope from which he pulled three black-and-white photographs. Clive turned the heat off under the saucepans and sat down. The first photograph Vernon put in his hands showed Julian Garmony in a plain three-quarter-length dress, posing cat–walk style, with arms pushing away a little from his body, and one foot set in front of the other, knees slightly crooked. The false breasts under the dress were small, and the edge of one bra strap was visible. The face was made up, but not overly so, for his natural pallor served him well, and lipstick had bestowed a bow of sensuality on the unkind, narrow lips. The hair was distinctively Garmony's, short, wavy and side-parted, so that his appearance was both manicured and dissolute, and faintly bovine. This was not something that could ever be passed off as fancy dress, or a lark in front of the camera. The strained, self-absorbed expression was that of a man revealed in a sexual state. The strong gaze into the lens was consciously seductive. The lighting was soft, and cleverly done.

'Molly,' Clive said, more to himself.

'You got it in one,' Vernon said. He was watching hungrily, waiting for a reaction, and it was partly to conceal his thoughts that Clive continued to gaze into the picture. What he felt first was simple relief, for Molly. A puzzle had been solved. This was what had drawn her to Garmony, the secret life, his vulnerability, the trust that must have bound them closer. Good old Molly. She would have been creative and playful, urging him on, taking him further into the dreams that the House of Commons could not fulfil, and he would have known that he could rely on her. If she had been ill in some other kind of way, she would have taken care to destroy these pictures. Had it ever moved beyond the bedroom? To restaurants in foreign cities? Two girls on the town. Molly would have known how. She knew the clothes and the places, and she would have adored the conspiracy and fun, the silliness and sexiness of it. Clive thought again how he loved her.

'Well?' Vernon said.

To forestall him, Clive put out a hand for another picture. In this, a head and shoulders shot, Garmony's dress was more silkily feminine. There was a simple line of lace around the high sleeves and neckline. Perhaps it was lingerie he was wearing. The effect was less successful, unmasking completely the lurking masculinity and revealing the pathos, the impossible hopes of his confounded identity. Molly's artful lighting could not dissolve the jaw bones of a huge head, or the swell of an Adam's apple. How he looked, and how he felt he looked, were probably very far apart. They should have been ridiculous, these photographs, they *were* ridiculous, but Clive was somewhat awed. We know so little about each other. We lie mostly submerged, like ice floes, with our visible social selves projecting only cool and white. Here was a rare sight below the waves, of a man's privacy and turmoil, of his dignity upended by the overpowering necessity of pure fantasy, pure thought, by the irreducible human element – mind.

For the first time Clive considered what it might be like to feel kindly towards Garmony. It was Molly who had made it possible. In the third of the pictures he wore a boxy Chanel jacket and his gaze was turned downwards; on some mental screen of selfhood he was a demure and feasible woman, but to an outsider what showed was evasion. Face it, you're a man. He was better off looking to camera, confronting us with his pretence.

'So?' Vernon was becoming impatient.

'Extraordinary.'

Clive handed the photographs back. He could not think clearly with the images still in his view. He said, 'So you're fighting to keep them out of the paper.'

It was part tease, part mischief, as well as a wish to delay voicing his thoughts.

Vernon was staring at him, amazed. 'Are you mad? This is the enemy. I just told you, we've got the injunction lifted.'

'Of course. Sorry. I wasn't quite with it.'

'My idea is to publish next week. What do you think?'

Clive tilted back on his chair and clasped his hands behind his head. 'I think,' he said carefully, 'I think your staff is right. It's a really terrible idea.'

'Meaning?'

'It'll ruin him.'

'Dead right it will.'

'I mean, personally.'

'Yup.'

There was a stalled silence. So many objections came crowding in on Clive that they seemed to cancel each other out.

Vernon pushed his empty glass across the table and as it was filled he said, 'I don't get it. He's pure poison. You've said so yourself many times.'

'He's vile,' Clive agreed.

'The word is he'll be mounting a leadership challenge in November. It would be terrible for the country if he was prime minister.'

'I think so too,' Clive said.

Vernon spread his hands. 'So?'

There was another pause while Clive stared up at the cracks in the ceiling, shaping his thoughts. At last he said, 'Tell me this. Do you think it's wrong in principle for men to dress up in women's clothes?'

Vernon groaned. He was beginning to behave like a drunk. He must have had a few before arriving. 'Oh, Clive!'

Clive kept on. 'You were once an apologist for the sexual revolution. You stood up for gays.'

'I don't believe I'm hearing this.'

'You stood up for plays and films that people wanted to ban. Only last year you spoke up for those cretins who were in court for hammering nails through their balls.'

Vernon winced. 'Penis actually.'

'Isn't this the kind of sexual expression you're so keen to defend? What exactly is Garmony's crime that needs to be exposed?'

'His hypocrisy, Clive. This is the hanger and flogger, the family values man, the scourge of immigrants, asylum seekers, travellers, marginal people.'

'Irrelevant,' Clive said.

'Of course it's relevant. Don't talk crap.'

'If it's OK to be a transvestite, then it's OK for a racist to be one. What's not OK is to be a racist.'

Vernon sighed in fake pity. 'Listen to me . . .'

But Clive had found his trope. 'If it's OK to be a transvestite, then it's OK for a family man to be one too. In private, of course. If it's OK to—'

'Clive! Listen to me. You're in your studio all day dreaming of symphonies. You've no idea what's at stake. If

Garmony's not stopped now, if he gets to be prime minister in November, they've got a good chance of winning the election next year. Another five years! There'll be even more people living below the poverty line, more people in prison, more homeless, more crime, more riots like last year. He's been speaking in favour of national service. The environment will suffer because he'd rather please his business friends than sign the accords on global warming. He wants to take us out of Europe. Economic catastrophe! It's all very fine for you' – here Vernon gestured around at the enormous kitchen – 'but for most people . . .'

'Careful,' Clive growled. 'When you're drinking my wine.' He reached for the Richebourg and filled Vernon's glass. 'A hundred and five pounds a bottle.'

Vernon downed half the glass. 'My point precisely. You're not becoming comfortable and right-wing in your middle age, are you?'

Clive answered the taunt with one of his own. 'You know what this is really about? You're doing George's work. He's setting you on. You're being used, Vernon, and I'm surprised you can't see through it. He hates Garmony for his affair with Molly. If he had something on me or you, he'd use that too.' Then Clive added, 'Perhaps he has. Did she take any of you? In the frogman's suit? Or was it the tutu? The people must be told.'

Vernon stood up and put the envelope back in his case. 'I came round hoping for your support. Or at the least, a sympathetic hearing. I didn't expect your fucking abuse.'

He went out into the hall. Clive followed him, but he did not feel apologetic.

Vernon opened the door and turned. He looked unwashed, wrecked. 'I don't get it,' he said quietly. 'I don't think you're being straight with me. What is it you really object to about this?'

Possibly the question was rhetorical. Clive took a couple of steps towards his friend and answered it. 'Because of Molly. We don't like Garmony, but she did. He trusted her, and she respected his trust. It was something private between them. These are her pictures, nothing to do with me or you or your readers. She would have hated what you're doing. Frankly, you're betraying her.'

Then, rather than let Vernon have the satisfaction of closing the door on him, Clive turned and walked away, towards the kitchen to eat his supper alone.

iii

Outside the hotel, set against a rough stone wall, was a long wooden bench. In the morning, after breakfast, Clive sat here to lace his boots. Although he was missing the key element of his finale, he had two important advantages in his search. The first was general: he felt optimistic. He had done the background work in his studio, and though he hadn't slept well, he was cheerful about being back in his favourite landscape. The second was specific: he knew exactly what he wanted. He was working backwards really, sensing that the theme lay in fragments and hints in what he had already written. He would recognise the right thing as soon as it occurred to him. In the finished piece the melody would sound to the innocent ear as though it had been anticipated or developed elsewhere in the score. Finding the notes would be an act of inspired synthesis. It was as if he knew them, but could not yet hear them. He knew their enticing sweetness and melancholy. He knew their simplicity, and the model, surely, was Beethoven's Ode to Joy. Consider the first line – a few steps up, a few steps down. It could be a nursery tune. It was completely without pretension, and yet carried such spiritual weight. Clive stood to receive his packed lunch from the waitress who had brought it out to him. Such was the exalted nature of his mission, and of his ambition. Beethoven. He

76

knelt on the car park gravel to stow in his daypack the grated cheese sandwiches.

He slung the pack across his shoulder and set off along the track into the valley. During the night a warm front had moved across the Lakes and already the frost had gone from the trees and from the meadow by the beck. The cloud cover was high and uniformly grey, the light was clear and flat, the path dry. Conditions did not come much better in late winter. He reckoned he had eight hours of daylight, though he knew that as long as he was off the fells and back down in the valley by dusk, he could find his way home with a torch. He had time then to climb Scafell Pike, but he could delay the decision until he was on Esk Hause.

During the first hour or so, after he had turned south into the Langstrath, he felt, despite his optimism, the unease of outdoor solitude wrap itself around him. He drifted helplessly into a daydream, an elaborate story about someone hiding behind a rock, waiting to kill him. Now and then he glanced over his shoulder. He knew this feeling well because he often hiked alone. There was always a reluctance to be overcome. It was an act of will, a tussle with instinct, to keep walking away from the nearest people, from shelter, warmth and help. A sense of scale habituated to the daily perspectives of rooms and streets was suddenly affronted by a colossal emptiness. The mass of rock rising above the valley was one long frown set in stone. The hiss and thunder of the stream was the language of threat. His shrinking spirit and all his basic inclinations told him that it was foolish and unnecessary to keep on, that he was making a mistake.

Clive kept on because the shrinking and apprehension were precisely the conditions – the sickness – from which he sought release, and proof that his daily grind – crouching over that piano for hours every day – had reduced him to a cringing state. He would be large again, and unafraid. There was no threat here, only elemental indifference. There were dangers of course, but only the usual ones, and mild enough; injury from a fall, getting lost, a violent change of weather, night. Managing these would restore him to a sense of control. Soon human meaning would be bleached from the rocks, the landscape would assume its beauty and draw him in; the unimaginable age of the mountains and the fine mesh of living things that lay across them would remind him that he was part of this order and insignificant within it, and he would be set free.

Today however, this beneficent process was taking longer than usual. He had been walking for an hour and a half and was still eyeing certain boulders ahead for what they might conceal, still regarding the sombre face of rock and grass at the end of the valley with vague dread, and still pestered by fragments of his conversation with Vernon. The open spaces that were meant to belittle his cares, were belittling everything: endeavour seemed pointless. Symphonies especially: feeble blasts, bombast, doomed attempts to build a mountain in sound. Passionate striving. And for what? Money. Respect. Immortality. A way of denying the randomness that spawned us, and of holding off the fear of death. He stopped to tighten his bootlaces. Further on he took off his sweater, and drank deeply from his water bottle, trying to eradicate the taste of the kipper he had unwisely eaten at breakfast. Then he found himself yawning, and thinking of the bed in his small room. But he could not possibly be tired already, nor could he turn back, not after all the efforts he had made to be here.

He came to a bridge across the stream and stopped to sit down. A decision had to be made. He could cross here and make a quick ascent up the left side of the valley to Stake Pass; or he could continue to the very end of the valley, then scramble up three hundred feet or so of steep slope to Tongue Head. He didn't really feel like a hand over hand scramble, but nor did he like the possibility that he might be giving in to weakness, or to age. Finally he decided to stay by the stream – the exertion of a climb might help jolt him out of his torpor.

An hour later he was at the end of the valley, facing the first steep incline and regretting his decision. It was beginning to rain hard, and whatever the claims made for the expensive waterproofs he was struggling into, he knew the physical effort of the climb was going to make him hot. Avoiding the slippery wet rock lower down, he picked a route over high, turfed banks and, sure enough, within minutes the sweat was pouring into his eyes, along with the rain. It bothered him that his pulse was so rapid so soon, and that he was pausing for breath every three or four minutes. An ascent like this should have been well within his powers. He drank from the water bottle and pushed on, taking advantage of his solitude to grunt and moan loudly at each difficult step.

With someone else along he might have made a joke of the humiliations of growing older. But these days he had no close friends in England who shared his compulsion. Everyone he knew seemed perfectly happy to get by without wilderness – a country restaurant, Hyde Park in spring, was all the open space they ever needed. Surely they could not claim to be fully alive. Hot, wet, panting, he strained to heave and lever himself onto a grassy ledge and lay there, cooling his face on the turf while the rain beat upon his back, and cursed his friends for their dullness, their lack of appetite for life. They had let him down. No one knew where he was, and no one cared.

After five minutes of listening to the rain rattling on the fabric of his waterproofs, he got to his feet and climbed on up. Anyway, was the Lake District really a wilderness? So eroded by walkers, with every last insignificant feature labelled and smugly celebrated. It was really nothing more than a gigantic brown gymnasium, and this incline just a set of grassy wall bars. This was a work-out, in the rain. More debilitating thoughts pursued him as he climbed towards the col, but as he gained height and the going became less steep, as the rain ceased and a long fissure in the cloud permitted a tiny consolation of diluted sunlight, it began to happen at last – he began to feel good. Perhaps it was no more than the effect of endorphins released by muscular exertion, or because he had simply found a rhythm. Or it might have been because this was a cherished moment in mountain walking, when one reached a col and began to cross the watershed, and new summits and valleys inched into view – Great End, Esk Pike, Bowfell. Now the mountains were beautiful.

On near level ground now, he strode across the tussocky grass towards the track that brought walkers up from Langdale. In summer this was a depressingly busy route, but today there was just a solitary hiker in blue crossing the broad fell, hurrying purposefully towards Esk Hause as though to a rendezvous. As he approached he saw it was a woman, prompting Clive to cast himself in the role of her man, in the assignation she seemed so keen to reach: waiting for her by a lonely tarn, calling her name as she approached, taking from his pack the champagne and two silver flutes, and going towards her . . . Clive had never had a lover, or even a wife, who liked hiking. Susie Marcellan, always game for something new, came to the Catskills with him once and turned out to be a helpless Manhattan exile, complaining comically all day long about bugs, blisters and the lack of cabs.

By the time he had reached the track the woman was half a mile ahead of him, and beginning to drift off to her right, towards Allen Crags. He stopped to let her go in order to have the great upland field to himself. The crack in the sky was opening further, and behind him, on Rosthwaite Fell, a baton of light across the bracken redeemed the reputation of the colour brown with fiery reds and yellows. He packed the waterproofs away, ate an apple and considered his route. He was for climbing Scafell Pike now, in fact he was impatient to set off. The quickest way up was from Esk Hause, but now that he had loosened up, he had it in mind to continue north-west, drop down to Sprinkling Tarn, and down again by Sty Head and make the long ascent by the Corridor Route. If he came down under Great End and went home the way he had come up, by the Langstrath, he would be at the hotel by dusk.

So he set off at an easy stride towards the broad enticing crest of Esk Hause, feeling that there was not really so much physical difference between him and his thirty-year-old self after all, and that it was not sinew but spirit that had held him back. How strong his legs felt now that his mood had improved!

Skirting the broad scars of erosion caused by hikers, he made a curving route to the ridge ahead of him and, as so often happened, thought about his life in fresh terms, gladdening himself with recollections of recent small successes: a reissue on disc of an early orchestral piece, a near-reverential mention of his work in a Sunday paper, the wise and humorous speech he had given when awarding the composition prize to a dumbstruck school-boy. Clive thought of his work in totality, of how varied and rich it seemed whenever he was able to raise his head and take the long perspective, how it represented in abstract a whole history of his lifetime. And still so much to do. He thought affectionately about the people in his life. Perhaps he had been too hard on Vernon, who was only trying to save his newspaper and protect the country from Garmony's harsh policies. He would phone Vernon this evening. Their friendship was too important to be lost to one isolated dispute. They could surely agree to differ and continue to be friends.

These benign thoughts brought him at last to the ridge where he had a view of the long descent towards Sty Head, and what he saw made him cry out in irritation. Spread out over more than a mile, marked by brilliant points of fluorescent oranges, blues and greens, was a party of walkers. They were schoolchildren, perhaps a hundred of them, filing down to the tarn. It would take him at least an hour to overtake them all. Instantly the landscape was transformed, tamed, reduced to a trampled beauty spot. Without giving himself time to dwell on old themes of his – the idiocy and visual pollution of day-glo anoraks, or why people were compelled to go about in such brutally large groups – he turned away to his right, towards Allen Crags, and the moment the party was out of sight he was restored to his good mood. He would spare himself the energetic ascent of Scafell Pike, and instead make a leisurely return along the ridge and down Thornythwaite Fell into the valley.

In a matter of minutes, it seemed, he was standing on top of the crag, regaining his breath and congratulating himself on his change of plan. He had before him a walk that Wainwright's *The Southern Fells* described as 'full of interest'; the path rose and fell by little tarns and crossed marshes, rocky outcrops and stony plateaus to reach the Glaramara summits. This was the prospect that had soothed him the week before as he was falling asleep.

He had been walking a quarter of an hour and was just climbing a slope that ended in a great tilted mottled rock slab when it finally happened, just as he had hoped it would: he was relishing his solitude, he was happy in his body, his mind was contentedly elsewhere, when he heard the music he had been looking for, or at least he heard a clue to its form.

It came as a gift; a large grey bird flew up with a loud alarm call as he approached. As it gained height and wheeled away over the valley it gave out a piping sound on three notes which he recognised as the inversion of a line he had already scored for a piccolo. How elegant, how simple. Turning the sequence round opened up the idea of a plain and beautiful song in common time which he could almost hear. But not quite. An image came to him of a set of unfolding steps, sliding and descending – from the trap door of a loft, or from the door of a light plane. One note lay over and suggested the next. He heard it, he had it, then it was gone. There was a glow of a tantalising after-image, and the fading call of a sad little tune. This synaesthesia was a torment. These notes were perfectly interdependent, little polished hinges swinging the melody through its perfect arc. He could almost hear it again as he reached the top of the angled rock slab and paused to reach into his pocket for notebook and pencil. It wasn't entirely sad. There was merriness there too, an optimistic resolve against the odds. Courage.

He was beginning to scribble out the fragments of what he had heard, hoping to will the rest into being, when he was aware of another sound, not imagined, not a bird call, but the murmur of a voice. He was so intent that he almost resisted the temptation to look up, but he could not help himself. Peering over the top of the slab that jutted up over a thirty-foot drop, he found himself looking down on a miniature tarn, hardly bigger than a large puddle. Standing on the grass that fringed it on its far side was the woman he had seen hurrying past, the woman in blue. Facing her, and talking in a low, constant drone, was a man who was certainly not dressed for rambling. His face was long and thin, like some snouty animal's. He wore an old tweed jacket and grey flannel trousers and a flat cloth cap, with a scrap of dirty white cloth wrapped round his neck. A hill farmer possibly, or a friend who disdained hiking and all the gear who had come up to meet her. The very assignation Clive had imagined.

This stark surprise, these vivid figures among the rocks, seemed to be there for his benefit alone. It was as if they were actors striking up a tableau whose meaning he was supposed to guess, as if they were not quite serious, only pretending not to know that he was watching. Whatever they were about, Clive's immediate thought was as clear as a neon sign: *I am not here.*

He ducked down and continued with his notes. If he could get the known elements on paper now, he could quietly remove himself to some place further along the ridge and work at the rest. He ignored the woman's voice when he heard it. Already it was hard to capture what had seemed so clear a minute before. For a while he floundered and then he had it again, that overlain quality, so obvious when it was before him, so elusive the moment his attention relaxed. He was crossing out notes as fast as he was setting them down, but when he heard the woman's voice rise to a sudden shout, his hand froze.

He knew it was a mistake, he knew he should have kept writing, but once again he peered over the rock. She had turned to face in Clive's direction now. He guessed her to be in her late thirties. She had a small, dark, boyish face and curly black hair. She and the man knew each other then, for they were arguing – a marital row, most likely. She had put her pack on the ground and was standing in an attitude of defiance, feet apart, hands on hips, head tilted slightly back. The man took a step towards her and seized her by the elbow. She shook him off with a sharp downward movement of her arm. Then she shouted something and picked up her pack, and tried to sling it across her shoulder. But he had hold of it too and was pulling. For a few seconds they tussled, and the pack was pulled this way and that. Then the man had it, and with a single contemptuous movement, a mere wave of the wrist, tossed it into the tarn where it bobbed half submerged, slowly sinking.

The woman took two quick paces into the water, then changed her mind. As she turned back the man made another attempt to take her arm. All this time they were talking, arguing, but the sound of their voices reached Clive only intermittently. He lay on his tilted slab, pencil between his fingers, notebook in his other hand, and sighed. Was he really going to intervene? He imagined running down there. The point at which he reached them was when the possibilities would branch: the man might run off; the woman would be grateful, and together they could descend to the main road by Seatoller. Even this least probable of outcomes would destroy his fragile inspiration. The man was more likely to redirect his aggression at Clive while the woman looked on, helpless. Or gratified, for that was possible too; they might be closely bound, they might both turn on him for presuming to interfere.

The woman shouted again and Clive, lying pressed against the rock, closed his eyes. Something precious, a little jewel, was rolling away from him. There had been another possibility; that instead of climbing up here, he had decided to go down to Sty Head, past the day-glo school children, to take the Corridor Route up Scafell Pike. Then, whatever was happening here was bound to take its course. Their fate, his fate. The jewel, the melody. Its momentousness pressed upon him. So much depended on it; the symphony, the celebration, his reputation, the lamented century's ode to joy. He did not doubt that what he half heard could bear the weight. In its simplicity lay all the authority of a lifetime's work. He also had no doubt that it was not a piece of music that was simply waiting to be discovered; what he had been doing, until interrupted, was *creating* it, forging it out of the call of a bird, taking advantage of the alert passivity of an engaged creating mind. What was clear now was the pressure of choice: he should either go down and protect the woman, if she needed protection, or he should creep away round the side of Glaramara to find a sheltered place to continue his work – if it was not already lost. He could not remain here doing nothing.

At the sound of an angry voice he opened his eyes and pulled himself up to take another look. The man had hold of her wrist and was trying to drag her round the tarn towards the shelter of the sheer rock face directly below Clive. She was scrabbling on the ground with her free hand, possibly looking for a stone to use as a weapon, but that only made it easier for him to jerk her along. Her backpack had sunk from sight. All the while he was talking to her, his voice having dropped again to its unceasing, indistinct drone. She made a sudden pleading whimpering sound and Clive knew exactly what it was he had to do. Even as he was easing himself back down the slope he understood that his hesitation had been a sham. He had decided at the very moment he was interrupted.

On level ground he hurried back along the way he had come, and then dropped down along the western side of the ridge in a long arc of detour. Twenty minutes later he found a flat-topped rock to use as a table and stood hunched over his scribble. There was almost nothing there now. He was trying to call it back but his concentration was being broken by another voice, the insistent, interior voice of self-justification: whatever it might have involved – violence, or the threat of violence, or his embarrassed apologies, or, ultimately, a statement to the police – if he had approached the couple, a pivotal moment in his career would have been destroyed. The melody could not have survived the psychic flurry. Given the width of the ridge and the numerous paths that crossed it, how easily he could have missed them. It was as if he wasn't there. He wasn't there. He was in his music. His fate, their fate, separate paths. It was not his business. This was his business, and it wasn't easy, and he wasn't asking for anyone's help.

At last he managed to calm himself and begin to work his way back. Here were the three notes of the bird call, here they were inverted for the piccolo, and here was the beginning of the overlapping, extending steps . . .

He stayed there for an hour, crouched above his writing. At last he put the notebook in his pocket and walked on at a quick pace, keeping all the while to the western side of the ridge, and soon dropping down to the fells. It took him three hours to reach the hotel and just as he did, the rain came on again. All the more reason then to cancel the rest of his stay and pack his bag and ask the waitress to call him a taxi. He had got what he wanted from the Lake District. He could work again on the train, and when he was home he would take this sublime sequence of notes and the lovely harmony he had written for it to the piano, and set free its beauty and sadness.

Surely it was creative excitement that made him pace up and down the cramped hotel bar waiting for his taxi, stopping now and then to gaze at the stuffed fox crouching in its evergreen foliage. It was excitement that caused him to step out into the lane a couple of times to see if his car was coming. He longed to be leaving the valley. When his taxi was announced, he hurried out and swung his bag onto the back seat, and told the driver to hurry. He wanted to be away, he was longing to be on a train, hurtling southwards, away from the Lakes. He wanted the anonymity of the city again, and the confinement of his studio, and – he had been thinking about this scrupulously – surely it was excitement that made him feel this way, not shame.

IV

i

Rose Garmony woke at six thirty and even before her eyes were open the names of three children were on her mind, on her mind's tongue: Leonora, John, Candy. Careful not to disturb her husband, she eased herself out of bed and reached for her dressing-gown. She had reread the notes last thing at night, and met Candy's parents in the afternoon. The other two cases were routine: a diagnostic bronchoscopy following the inhalation of a peanut, and the insertion of a chest drain for a lung abscess. Candy was a quiet little West Indian girl whose hair had been kept back-combed and ribboned by her mother all through the dreary routines of a long illness. The open-heart procedure would last least three hours, possibly five, and the outcome was uncertain. The father ran a grocery in Brixton and brought to the meeting a basket of pineapples, mangoes and grapes – propitiation for the savage god of the knife.

The scent of this fruit filled the kitchen now as Mrs Garmony entered barefoot to fill the kettle. While it heated she crossed the apartment's narrow hallway to her office and packed her briefcase, pausing to glance at the notes once more. She returned a call to the party chairman, after which she wrote a note to her grown-up son who was asleep in the guest room, then she went back to the kitchen to make the tea. She took her cup to the kitchen window and, without moving the lace curtain, looked down into the street. She counted eight of them on the pavement of Lord North Street, three more than were there the same time yesterday. There was no sign yet of the TV cameras, or of the policemen the Home Secretary had personally promised. She should have made Julian stay over at Carlton Gardens, rather than here, in her old flat. They were supposed to be competitors, these people, but they stood in a loose, chatty group, like men outside a pub on a summer's evening. One of them was kneeling on the ground, attaching something to an aluminium pole. Then he stood and scanned the windows and seemed to see her. She watched, expressionlessly, as a camera came bobbing and telescoping towards her. When it was almost level with her face she stepped back from the window and went upstairs to dress.

A quarter of an hour later she took another peep, this time from the sitting-room window, two floors up. She felt just as she liked to be before a difficult day at the children's hospital: calm, alert, impatient to begin the work. No guests the night before, no wine at supper, an hour with the notes, seven hours' unbroken sleep. She would let nothing break this mood, so she stared down at the group – there were nine of them now – with controlled fascination. The man had collapsed his extendable pole and had rested it against the railings. One of the others was bringing a tray of coffees from the take-away shop on Horseferry Road. What could they ever hope to get that they didn't already have? And so early in the morning.

What sort of satisfaction could they have from this kind of work? And why was it they looked so alike, these doorsteppers, as though drawn from one tiny gene puddle of humanity? Large-faced, jowly, pushy men in leather jackets who spoke with the same accent, an odd blend of fake Cockney and fake posh, which they delivered with the same pleading, belligerent whine. 'Ere, this way please, Mrs Garmony! Rose!

Fully dressed now and ready to leave, she carried his tea and the morning papers into the darkened bedroom. She hesitated at the foot of the bed. Lately his days had been so vile, she was reluctant to wake him into another one. He had driven from Wiltshire last night, then stayed up late sipping Scotch, she knew, in front of a video of Bergman's *The Magic Flute*. Then he pulled out all Molly Lane's letters, the ones that stupidly indulged his grotesque cravings. Thank God that episode was over, thank God the woman was dead. The letters were still spread out over the carpet and he would need to put them away before the cleaning lady came. Only the top of his head was visible on the pillow – fifty-two, and his hair still black. She ruffled it gently. Sometimes, on the rounds, a nurse might wake a child for her this way, and Rose was always touched by those seconds of confusion in some small boy's eyes as he grasped that he was not at home and that the touch was not his mother's.

'Darling,' she whispered.

His voice was muffled by the winter duvet. 'Are they out there?'

'Nine of them.'

'Fuck.'

'I've got to run. I'll phone you. Take this.'

He pushed the bedclothes clear of his face and sat up. 'Of course. The little girl. Candy. Good luck.'

They kissed lightly on the lips as she put the cup in his hands. She laid her hand on his cheek and reminded him of the letters on the floor. Then she stepped away quietly and went downstairs to phone her secretary at the hospital. In the hall she put on a thick woollen overcoat, checked herself in the mirror, and was about to pick up her case, keys and scarf when she changed her mind and went back up. She found him as she guessed she would, on his back, arms outspread, dozing, the tea cooling by a pile of departmental memos. There hadn't been time in the past week, with the crisis, and the photos to be published tomorrow, Friday, there simply hadn't been a moment when she'd been able or wanted to discuss her cases with him, and though she knew it was an old politician's skill, remembering the names, she was touched that he'd made the effort. She tapped his hand and whispered.

'Julian.'

'Oh God,' he said without opening his eyes. 'First meeting's at half eight. Got to walk past the snakes.'

She spoke in the voice she used to calm desperate parents; slow, light, airy rather than grave. 'It's going to be fine, perfectly fine.'

He smiled at her, completely unconvinced. She leaned over and spoke into his ear. 'Trust me.'

Downstairs, she checked herself in the mirror once more. She buttoned her coat full, and arranged the scarf to half conceal her face. She picked up her case and let herself out of the flat. Down in the entrance hall she paused by the front door with her hand on the lock, preparing herself to open it and make a dash for her car.

'Oi! Rosy! This way! Looking sad now please, Mrs Garmony.'

About the same time, three miles to the west, Vernon Halliday was waking from, then tumbling back into, dreams of running, or memories of running vivified by their dream-like form, dream-memories of running down corridors of dusty red carpet towards a boardroom, *late*, late again, late to the point of apparent contempt, running from the last meeting to this, with seven more to get through before lunch, outwardly walking, inwardly sprinting, all week long, laying out the arguments before the furious grammarians, and then *The Judge*'s sceptical board of directors, its production staff, its lawyers and then his own, and then George Lane's people and the Press Council and a live television audience and innumerable, unmemorable airless radio studios. Vernon made his public-interest case for publishing the photographs much as he had made it to Clive, but sleekly, at greater length and speed, with more urgency and definition and proliferating examples, with pie charts, block graphs and spreadsheets and soothing precedents. But mostly he was running, weaving dangerously towards taxis across crowded streets, and out of taxis across marbled foyers and into lifts, and out of lifts along corridors that sloped exasperatingly upwards, slowing him down, making him later. He woke briefly and noted that his wife, Mandy, had already left the bed, then his eyes were closing and he was back there again, lifting his briefcase high as he waded through water, or blood, or tears coursing over a red carpet that brought him to an amphitheatre where he mounted a podium to make his case while all around him was a silence that towered like redwoods, and in the gloom, dozens of averted eyes, and someone walking away from him across the circus sawdust who looked like Molly but would not answer when he called.

At last he woke fully into the calm of morning sounds – birdsong, the distant radio in the kitchen, the soft closing of a cupboard door. He pushed the covers away and lay on his back naked, feeling the centrally heated air drying the clamminess on his chest. His dreams were simply a kaleidoscopic fracturing of his week, fair comment on its pace and emotional demands, but omitting – with the unthinking partisan bias of the unconscious – the game-plan, the rationale whose evolving logic had in fact kept him sane. Publication day was tomorrow, Friday, with one picture held over to Monday to keep the story alive. And the story seethed with life, it had kicking legs and was running even faster than Vernon. For days, since the injunction had been lifted, *The Judge* had trailed the Garmony story, stroking and fine-tuning public curiosity so that photographs no one had ever seen had become an icon in the political culture, from Parliament to pub, an item of general discussion, a subject on which no important player could afford to be without an opinion. The paper had covered the courtroom battles, the icy support of fraternal government colleagues, the dithering of the

Prime Minister, the 'grave concern' of senior Opposition figures and the musings of the great and the good. *The Judge* had thrown open its pages to denunciations by those opposed to publication, and it had sponsored a televised debate on the need for a privacy law.

Despite the dissenting voices, a broad consensus was emerging that *The Judge* was a decent, fighting paper, and that the government had been in power too long and was financially, morally and sexually corrupt, and that Julian Garmony was typical of it, and was a despicable person whose head was urgently needed on a plate. In a week, sales were up by a hundred thousand, and the editor was finding he was arguing into silence from his senior editors rather than protests; secretly they all wanted him to go ahead as long as their principled dissent was minuted. Vernon was winning the argument because everyone, lowly journalists included, now saw they could have it both ways – their paper saved, their consciences unstained.

He stretched, shuddered, yawned. There were seventy-five minutes before the first meeting and soon he would get up to shave and shower, but not yet, not while he was holding on to the day's only tranquil moment. His nakedness against the sheet, the wanton tangle of bed-clothes by his ankle and the sight of his own genitalia, at his age not yet fully obscured by the swell and spread of his gut, sent vague sexual thoughts floating across his mind like remote summer clouds. But Mandy would be just leaving for work, and his latest friend, Dana, who worked at the House of Commons, was abroad until Tuesday. He rolled onto his side and wondered whether he had it in him to masturbate, whether it might serve him well to have his mind cleared for the business ahead. He made a few absent-minded strokes, then gave up. These days he seemed to lack the dedication and clarity or emptiness of mind, and the action itself seemed quaintly outmoded and improbable, like lighting a fire by rubbing two sticks.

Besides, in Vernon's life lately, there was so much to think about, so much of the real world that thrilled, that mere fantasy could hardly compete. What he had said, what he would say, how it went down, the next move, the unravelling consequences of success . . . In the accumulating momentum of the week, practically every hour had revealed to Vernon new aspects of his powers and potential, and as his gifts for persuasion and planning began to produce results, he felt large and benign, a little ruthless perhaps but ultimately good, capable of standing alone, against the current, seeing over the heads of his contemporaries, knowing that he was about to shape the destiny of his country and that he could bear the responsibility. More than bear – he *needed* this weight, his gifts needed the weight that no one else could shoulder. Who else could have moved so decisively when George, concealing his identity behind an agent, went on the open market with the pictures? Eight other newspapers put in bids and Vernon had to quadruple the original price to secure the deal. It seemed strange to him now that not so long ago he had been afflicted by a numbness of the scalp and a sense of not existing that had provoked in him fears of madness and death. Molly's funeral had given him the jitters. Now his purpose and being filled him to his fingertips. The story was alive, and so was he.

But one small matter denied him complete happiness: Clive. He had addressed him in his mind so often, sharpening the arguments, adding all the things he should have said that night, that he could almost convince himself that he was winning his old friend round, just as he was triumphing over the dinosaurs on the board of directors. But they hadn't spoken since their row, and Vernon was worrying more as publication day approached. Was Clive brooding, or furious, or was he locked in his studio, lost in work and oblivious to public affairs? Several times during the week Vernon had thought of snatching a minute alone to phone him. But he worried that a fresh attack from Clive would unsteady him in the meetings ahead. Now Vernon eyed the bedside phone beyond the heaped and buckled pillows, and then he made a lunge. Best not let forethought make a coward of him again. He had to save this friendship. Best to do it while he was calm. He already had a ring tone when he noticed it was only eight fifteen. Way too early. Sure enough, something in the fumble and clatter of Clive's pick-up suggested the near-paraplegia of shattered sleep.

'Clive? It's Vernon.'

'What?'

'Vernon. I woke you. I'm sorry . . .'

'No, no. Not at all. I was just standing here, just thinking . . .'

There was a rustle of sheets in the receiver while Clive rearranged himself in his bed. Why did we so often lie about sleep on the phone? Was it our vulnerability we defended? When he came on again his voice wasn't quite so thick.

'I've been meaning to phone you, but I've got rehearsals in Amsterdam next week. I've been working so hard.'

'Me too,' Vernon said. 'I haven't had a spare minute this week. Look, I wanted to talk to you again about those photographs.'

There was a pause. 'Oh yes. Those. I suppose you're going ahead.'

'I've canvassed a lot of opinion and the consensus is that we should publish. Tomorrow.'

Clive cleared his throat softly. He really did sound remarkably relaxed about it. 'Well, I've said my say. We'll just have to agree to differ.'

Vernon said, 'I wouldn't want it to come between us.'

'Of course not.'

The conversation moved on to other things. Naturally, Vernon gave a rather general account of his week. Clive told him how he'd been working through the nights, and how he was making great progress with the symphony, and what a good idea it had been, to go walking in the Lake District.

'Oh yes,' Vernon said. 'How was that?'

'I walked over this place called Allen Crags. That's where I had the breakthrough, pure inspiration, this melody you see . . .'

It was at this point that Vernon became aware of the call-waiting bleep. Twice, three times, then it stopped. Someone from his office. Probably Frank Dibben. The day, the last and most important day, was getting into gear. He sat naked on the edge of the bed and snatched up his watch to check it against the alarm clock. Clive wasn't angry with him so that was fine, and now he needed to get going.

'. . . they couldn't see me from where I was and it was looking nasty, but I had to make a decision . . .'

'Mmm,' Vernon repeated every half minute or so. He was right out at the end of the stretched telephone cord, standing on one foot, reaching with the other for clean underwear from a pile. The shower was out. So was the wet shave.

'. . . and he might have beaten her to a pulp for all I know. But then again . . .'

'Mmm.'

With the phone wedged between his shoulder and the side of his head, he was trying to ease a shirt out of its cellophane wrapper without making a din. Was it boredom or sadism that made the shirt service people do up every single button?

'. . . about half a mile away and found this rock, sort of used it as a table . . .'

Vernon was halfway into his trousers when the call-waiting sounded again. 'Absolutely,' he said. 'A rock table. Anyone in their right mind would use one. But Clive, I'm late for work. Gotta run. How about a drink tomorrow?'

'Oh. Oh all right. Fine. Drop by after work.'

iii

Vernon extricated himself from the back of the tiny car his paper allowed him and paused on the pavement outside Judge House to straighten his rumpled suit. As he hurried across the black and ginger marble vestibule he saw Dibben waiting by the lift. Frank had become deputy foreign editor on his twenty-eighth birthday. Four years and three editors later, he was still there and rumoured to be restless. They called him Cassius for his lean and hungry look, but this was unfair: his eyes were dark, his face long and pale, his stubble heavy, giving him the appearance of a police cell interrogator, but his manner was courteous, though a little withdrawn, and he had an attractive, wry intelligence. Vernon had always detested him in an absent-minded way, but had come round to Frank in the early days of the Garmony turmoil. The evening after the Chapel passed its no confidence vote in the editor, the evening after Vernon's compact with Clive, the young man stalked Vernon's hunched figure down the street at dusk and finally approached, touched his shoulder and suggested a drink. There was something persuasive in Dibben's tone.

They stepped into a side-street pub unknown to Vernon, a place of torn red plush and dim smoky air, and took a booth right at the back behind a giant jukebox. Over gin and tonics Frank confessed to his editor his quiet outrage at the way things had turned out. Last night's vote had been manipulated by the usual Chapel suspects whose beefs and feuds stretched back years, and he, Frank, had stayed away from the meeting pleading pressure of work. There were others, he said, who felt the same way, who wanted *The Judge* to broaden its appeal and get lively and do something bold like stitching up Garmony, but the dead hand of the grammarians was on every lever of patronage and promotion. The old guard would rather see the paper die than let it reach out to an under-thirties readership. They had fought off the bigger typeface, the lifestyle section, the horoscope, the complementary health supplement, the gossip column, the virtual bingo and the agony uncle, as well as snappy coverage of the Royal Family and pop music. Now they were turning on the one editor who could save *The Judge*. Among the younger staff there was support for Vernon, but it didn't have a voice. No one wanted to stand up first and be shot down.

Feeling suddenly light on his feet, Vernon went to the bar for another round. Clearly, it was time he started listening to his junior staff, time he brought them on. Back at the table Frank lit a cigarette and politely turned in his chair to blow his smoke out of the booth. He accepted the drink and continued. Of course, he hadn't seen the pictures, but he knew it must be right to run them. He wanted to give Vernon his support, and more than that. He wanted to be of use, which was why it wouldn't be right for him to be openly identified as the editor's ally. He excused himself and went to the food counter to order sausage and mash, and Vernon imagined a bedsit or studio flat, and no one there, no girl waiting for the deputy foreign editor to come home.

When Frank sat down again he said in a rush, 'I could keep you in touch. I could let you know what they're saying. I could find out where your real support is. But I'd have to look uninvolved, neutral. Would you mind that?'

Vernon did not commit himself. He had been around too long to let himself sign up an office spy without knowing more. He turned the conversation towards Garmony's politics and the two passed an agreeable half hour exploring a shared contempt. But three days later, when Vernon was beginning to run the corridors, startled by the frenzy of opposition and starting – but just slightly – to waver, he returned with Dibben to the same pub, to exactly the same booth, and showed him the photographs. The effect was heartening. Frank gazed at each one at length, without comment, simply shaking his head. Then he put them back in the envelope and said quietly, 'Incredible. The hypocrisy of the man.'

They sat in thoughtful silence a moment, then he added, 'You have to do it. You mustn't let them stop you. It'll wreck his chances for PM. It'll finish him completely. Vernon, I really want to help.'

The support among the younger staff was never quite as identifiable as Frank had claimed, but during the days it took to bring *The Judge* as a whole to quiescence, it was invaluable to know which arguments were hitting the mark. Through his rendezvous behind the jukebox he learned when and why the opposition was beginning to divide and when to press home his points. During the planning and execution of the build-up, Vernon knew exactly whom to isolate and work on among the grammarians. He was able to bounce ideas for the build-up off Frank, who came up with some good suggestions of his own. Most of all, Vernon had someone to talk to, someone who shared his sense of historical mission and excitement, and instinctively understood the momentous nature of the affair, and who offered encouragement when everyone else was so critical.

With the managing director on board and the build-ups and trails written, with circulation rising and a muted but unforgiving excitement trickling through the staff, the meetings with Frank had no longer been necessary. But Vernon was looking to reward his loyalty and had it in mind to put him up for Lettice's job, features editor. Her foot-dragging over the Siamese twins had put her on probation. The chess supplement had been her death warrant.

Now, this Thursday morning, the last day before publication, Vernon and his lieutenant rose together to the fourth floor in an ancient lift that seemed to have the jitters. Vernon was taken back to his undergraduate acting days, the final rehearsal, the sticky palms and swooping gut and loose bowels. By the time the morning conference ended, all the senior editorial staff, all the senior journalists and quite a few more besides, would have seen the photographs. The first edition went to press at 5.15, but not until 9.30, the late edition, would Garmony's image, his frock and his soulful gaze, be a furious blur on the steel rollers at the new Croydon plant. The idea was to deny the competition any chance of running a spoiler for their own late editions. The distribution lorries would be on the road by 11.00. Then it would be too late to recall the deed.

'You saw the press,' Vernon said.

'Pure bliss.'

Today all the papers, broadsheets and all, had been obliged to run related features. You could see the reluctance and the envy in every caption, in every busily researched fresh angle. The *Independent* had come up with a tired piece on privacy laws in ten different countries. The *Telegraph* had a psychologist theorising pompously on cross-dressing, and the *Guardian* had given over a double-page spread, dominated by a picture of J. Edgar Hoover in a cocktail dress, to a sneering, wised-up piece on transvestites in public life. None of these papers could bring itself to mention *The Judge*. The *Mirror* and the *Sun* had concentrated on Garmony at his farm in Wiltshire. Both papers displayed similar grainy long-lens photos of the Foreign Secretary and his son disappearing into the darkness of a barn. The huge doors gaped wide, and the way the light fell across Garmony's shoulders, but not his arms, suggested a man about to be swallowed up by obscurity.

Between the second and third floors Frank punched a button to brake the winching mechanism, and stopped the lift with a horrible jolt that clutched at Vernon's heart. The ornate brass and mahogany box creaked as it swayed above the shaft. They had held a couple of quick conferences like this before. The editor felt obliged to conceal his terror and appear nonchalant.

'Just briefly,' Frank said. 'McDonald will be giving a little speech at conference. Not quite saying they were wrong, not quite forgiving you either. But you know, congratulations all round and since we're going ahead, let's pull together.'

'Fine,' Vernon said. It would be exquisite, listening to the deputy editor apologise without appearing to do so.

'Thing is, others might chime in, there might even be some applause, that sort of thing. If it's all right with you, I think I should hang back, not show my hand at this stage.'

Vernon felt a faint, brief inner disturbance, like the tightening of some neglected reflexive muscle. He was touched by curiosity as much as distrust, but it was too late to do anything now, so he said, 'Sure. I need you in place. The next few days could be crucial.'

Frank hit the button and for a moment nothing happened. Then the lift plummeted a few inches before lurching upwards.

As usual, Jean was on the other side of the concertina gates with her bundle of letters, faxes and briefing notes.

'They're waiting for you in room six.'

The first meeting was with the advertising manager and his team who felt this was the moment to hike the rates. Vernon wanted to hang back. As they hurried along the corridor – red carpeted as in his dreams – he noticed Frank peel away just as two others joined them, people from layout. There was pressure to crop the front page picture to make way for a longer standfirst, but Vernon had already made up his mind about the copy he wanted. The obituaries editor, Manny Skelton, scuttled sideways out of his cupboard-sized office and pushed a few pages of typescript into Vernon's hand as he strode by. This would be the piece they had commissioned in case Garmony topped himself. The letters editor joined the throng, hoping for a word before the first meeting began. He was anticipating a deluge and was fighting for a whole page. Now, as he paced towards room six, Vernon was himself again, large, benign, ruthless and good. Where others would have felt a weight upon their shoulders, he felt an enabling lightness, or indeed a light, a glow of competence and well-being, for his sure hands were about to cut away a cancer from the organs of the body politic – this was the image he intended to use in the leader that would follow Garmony's resignation. Hypocrisy would be exposed, the country would stay in Europe, capital punishment and compulsory conscription would remain a crank's dream, social welfare would survive in some form or other, the global environment would get a decent chance, and Vernon was on the point of breaking into song.

He didn't, but the next two hours had all the brio of a light opera in which every aria was his, and in which a shifting chorus of mixed voices both praised him and harmoniously echoed his thoughts. Then it was eleven o'clock and far more than the usual number were cramming into Vernon's office for the morning conference. There were editors and their deputies and assistants and journalists crammed into every chair, slouched against every inch of wall space and perched along the window sills and on the radiators. People who could not squeeze into the room were bunched around the open doorway. Conversation stopped as the editor edged himself into his chair. It was positively raffish, the way he started without preamble, as always, and stuck to the routine – a few minutes' post-mortem, then a run through the lists. Today, of course, there would be no bids for the front page. Vernon's one concession was to reverse the usual order so that home news and politics would be last. The sports editor had a background piece on the Atlanta Olympics and a why-oh-why on the state of English table tennis doubles. The literary editor, who had never before been in early enough to attend a morning conference, gave a somnolent account of a novel about food which sounded so pretentious that Vernon had to cut him off. From arts there was a funding crisis, and Lettice O'Hara in features was at last ready to run her piece on the Dutch medical scandal, and also, to honour the occasion, was offering a feature on how industrial pollution was turning male fish into females.

When the foreign editor spoke, attention in the room began to focus. There was a meeting of European foreign ministers and Garmony would be attending – unless he resigned straight away. With this possibility floated, a murmur of excitement spread through the room. Vernon brought in the political editor, Harvey Straw, who dilated on the history of political resignations. There hadn't been many lately and it clearly was a dying art. The Prime Minister, well known to be strong on personal friendship and loyalty, weak on political instinct, was likely to hang on to Garmony until he was forced out. This would prolong the affair, which could only help *The Judge*.

At Vernon's invitation, the circulation manager confirmed the latest figures which were the best in seventeen years. At this, the murmur swelled to a clamour and there was some swaying and stumbling around the doorway as frustrated journalists standing in Jean's outer office decided to push against a wall of bodies. Vernon slapped the table to bring the room to order. They had still to hear from Jeremy Ball, the home editor, who was obliged to raise his voice; a ten-year-old boy was going on trial today accused of murder; the Lakeland rapist had struck for a second time in a week and a man was arrested last night; there was an oil spill off the coast of Cornwall. But no one was really interested, for there was only one subject that would quieten this crowd, and finally Ball obliged; a letter to the *Church Times* from a bishop attacking *The Judge* over the Garmony affair ought to be dealt with in today's leader; there was a meeting of the government's backbench committee this afternoon which should be covered; a brick had been thrown through the window of Garmony's constituency headquarters in Wiltshire. Ragged applause followed this news, and then silence as Grant McDonald, Vernon's deputy, started in on his few words.

He was an old timer on *The Judge*, a large man whose face was almost lost inside a ridiculous red beard he never trimmed. He liked to make great play of being a Scot, wearing a kilt to the Burns' Night he organised for the paper, and honking on bagpipes at the New Year's office party. Vernon suspected McDonald had never been further north than Muswell Hill. In public he had given due support to his editor, and in private, with Vernon, he had been sceptical of the whole affair. Somehow the entire building seemed to know about his scepticism which was why he was listened to so eagerly now. He started at a low growl which intensified the silence around him.

'I can say this now and it'll come as a surprise to you, but I've had my wee doubts about this right from the start . . .'

This disingenuous opener earned him a manly round of laughter. Vernon thrilled to the dishonesty of it; the matter was rich, complex, byzantine. There came to his mind an image of a burnished plate of beaten gold inscribed with faded hieroglyphs.

McDonald went on to describe his doubts – personal privacy, tabloid methods, hidden agendas and so on. Then he came to the hinge of his speech and raised his voice. Frank's briefing was spot on.

'But I've learned over the years that there are times in this business – not many, mind – when your own opinions have to take a back seat. Vernon's made his case with a passion and a deadly journalistic instinct, and there's a feeling in this building, an urgency on this paper now, that takes me back to the good old times of the three-day week when we really knew how to tell it. Today the circulation figures speak for themselves – we've tapped the public mood. So . . .' Grant turned to the editor and beamed. 'We're riding high again and it's all down to you. Vernon, a thousand thanks!'

After the loud applause, others chimed in with brief

messages of congratulation. Vernon sat with folded arms, his face solemn, his gaze fixed on the grain in the table's veneer. He wanted to smile, but it wouldn't seem right. He observed with satisfaction that the managing director, Tony Montano, was discreetly taking notes of who was saying what. Who was on board. He would have to be taken aside and reassured about Dibben who had slumped down in his chair, hands deep in his pockets, frowning and shaking his head.

Now Vernon stood for the benefit of those at the back of the room and returned the thanks. He knew, he said, that most people in the room had been against publication at one time or another. But he was grateful for this because in some respects journalism resembled science: the best ideas were the ones that survived, and were strengthened by, intelligent opposition. This fragile conceit prompted a hearty round of applause; no need for shame then, or retribution from on high. By the time the clapping faded, Vernon had squeezed through the crowd to a whiteboard mounted on the wall. He peeled away the masking tape that held in place a large sheet of blank paper and revealed a double size blow-up of tomorrow's front page.

The photograph filled the entire width of eight columns, and ran from under the masthead to three-quarters of the way down the page. The silent room took in the simply cut dress, the cat-walk fantasy, the sassy pose that playfully, enticingly, pretended to repel the camera's gaze, the tiny breasts and artfully revealed bra strap, the faint blush of make-up on the cheekbones, the lipstick's caress that moulded the swell and semi-pout of the mouth, the intimate, yearning look of an altered but easily recognisable public face. Centred below, in thirty-two-point lower-case bold, was a single line: 'Julian Garmony, Foreign Secretary'. There was nothing else on the page.

The crowd that had been so boisterous was completely subdued now, and the silence lasted for over half a minute. Then Vernon cleared his throat and began to describe the strategy for Saturday and Monday. As one young journalist would remark to another later in the canteen, it was like seeing someone you know stripped in public and flogged. Unmasked and punished. Despite this, the general view that took hold as people dispersed and returned to their desks, and consolidated in the early afternoon, was that this was work of the highest professional standards. As a front page it would surely become a classic which one day would be taught in journalism school. The visual impact was unforgettable, as was the simplicity, the starkness, the power. McDonald was right, Vernon's instinct was unerring. He was thinking only of the jugular when he pushed all the copy on to page two, and resisted the temptation of a screaming headline or a wordy caption. He knew the strength of what he had. He let the picture tell the story.

When the last person had left his office, Vernon closed the door and dispelled the fug by pushing the windows open wide to the damp March air. He had five minutes before his next meeting and he needed to think. He told Jean over the intercom that he was not to be disturbed. The thought scrolled round and round in his mind – it went well, it went well. But there was something, something important, some new information he had been about to respond to, then he was diverted, and then he forgot, it flashed away from him in a swarm of other similar items. It was a remark, a snippet that surprised him at the time. He should have spoken up right then.

In fact it didn't come until the late afternoon when he had another chance alone. He stood by the whiteboard trying to taste again that fleeting flavour of surprise. He closed his eyes and set about remembering the morning conference in sequence, everything that was said. But he could not keep his thoughts on the task and he drifted. It was going well, it was going well. But for this one little thing he would be hugging himself, he would be dancing on the desk. It was rather like this morning when he lay in bed contemplating his successes, denied full happiness by the single fact of Clive's disapproval.

And there he had it. Clive. The moment he thought of his friend's name, it came back to him. He went across the room towards the phone. It was simple, and possibly outrageous.

'Jeremy? Could you step into my office for a moment?'

Jeremy Ball was with him in less than a minute. Vernon sat him down and began an interrogation and took notes on places, dates, times, what was known, what was suspected. At one point Ball used the phone to confirm details with the journalist covering the story. Then, as soon as the home editor had left, Vernon used his private line to call Clive. Again, the protracted, clattering pick-up, the sound of bedclothes, the cracked voice. It was past four o'clock, so what was it with Clive, lying there all day like a depressed teenager?

'Ah, Vernon, I was just . . .'

'Look, something you said this morning. I need to ask you. What day was it you were in the Lake District?'

'Last week.'

'Clive, it's important. What day?'

There was a grunt and a creak as Clive struggled to pull himself upright.

'It would have been Friday. What's the . . . ?'

'The man you saw, no, wait. What time were you on this Allen Crags?'

'About one, I'd say.'

'Listen. The guy you saw attacking this woman, and you decided not to help her. It was the Lakeland rapist.'

'Never heard of him.'

'Don't you ever read the papers? He's attacked eight women in the last year, mostly hikers. As it happened, this one got away.'

'That's a relief.'

'No, it isn't. He attacked someone two days ago. They arrested him yesterday.'

'Well that's all right then.'

'No, it isn't all right. You didn't want to help this woman. Fine. But if you'd've gone to the police afterwards this other woman wouldn't have copped it.'

There was a brief pause as Clive took this in, or gathered himself. Now he was fully awake and his voice had hardened.

He said, 'That doesn't follow, but never mind. Why are you raising your voice, Vernon? Is this one of your manic days? What exactly do you want?'

'I want you to go to the police now and tell them what you saw . . .'

'Out of the question.'

'You could identify this man.'

'I'm in the final stages of finishing a symphony which . . .'

'No you're not, dammit. You're in bed.'

'That's none of your business.'

'This is outrageous. Go to the police, Clive. It's your moral duty.'

An audible intake of breath, another pause as though for reconsideration, then, 'You're telling me my moral duty? You? Of all people?'

'Meaning what?'

'Meaning these photographs. Meaning crapping on Molly's grave . . .'

The excremental reference to a non-existent burial place marked that point in a dispute when a corner is turned and all restraints are off. Vernon cut in. 'You know nothing, Clive. You live a privileged life and you know fuck all about anything.'

'. . . Meaning hounding a man from office. Meaning gutter journalism. How can you live with yourself?'

'You can bluster all you want. You're losing your grip. If you won't go to the police, I'll phone them myself and tell them what you saw. Accessory to an attempted rape . . .'

'Have you gone mad? How dare you threaten me!'

'There are certain things more important than symphonies. They're called people.'

'And are these people as important as circulation figures, Vernon?'

'Go to the police.'

'Fuck off.'

'No. You fuck off.'

The door of Vernon's office opened suddenly and Jean was there, writhing with anxiety. 'I'm sorry to interrupt a private conversation, Mr Halliday,' she said. 'But I think you better turn on the television. Mrs Julian Garmony is giving a press conference. Channel One.'

The Party managers thought long and hard about the matter and made some reasonable decisions. One was to allow cameras into a well-known children's hospital that morning to film Mrs Garmony emerging from the operating theatre, tired but happy, after performing open-heart surgery on a nine-year-old black girl called Candy. The surgeon was also filmed on her rounds, followed by respectful nurses and registrars, and being hugged by children who clearly adored her. Then, captured briefly in the hospital car park was a tearful encounter between Mrs Garmony and the little girl's grateful parents. These were the first images Vernon saw after he had slammed down the phone, searched in vain for the remote control among the papers on his desk, and bounded across to the monitor mounted high in a corner of his office. While the sobbing father heaped half a dozen pineapples into the arms of the surgeon, a voice-over explained that one could rise so high in the medical hierarchy for it to become inappropriate to be addressed as 'doctor'. It was Mrs Garmony to you.

Vernon, whose heart was still thudding from the row, retreated to his desk to watch while Jean tiptoed away, closing the door quietly behind her. Now we were in Wiltshire, at some elevated point, gazing down at a little tree-lined stream threading its way between the bald and undulating hills. There was a cosy farmhouse nestling by the trees, and as the commentary sketched in the familiar background to the Garmony affair, the camera began a long, slow zoom which ended on a sheep tending its newborn lamb on the front lawn, close to the shrubbery, right by the front door. It was another Party decision to send the Garmonys and their two grown-up children, Annabel and Ned, to their country home for a long weekend as soon as Rose was finished at the hospital. Vernon saw them now as a family group, looking towards camera over a five-barred gate, dressed in woollies and oil-cloth coats and accompanied by their sheepdog Milly and the family cat, a British Short Hair by the name of Brian, which Annabel lovingly cradled. It was a photo-call, but the Foreign Secretary was uncharacteristically hanging back, looking, well, sheepish, even lambish, for his wife was the centre of this event. Vernon knew that Garmony was sunk, but he could not help but nod in knowing tribute to the presentational skills, the sheer professionalism of it all.

The commentary faded and there was actual sound, the snap and whirr of motor-driven still cameras and various aggrieved voices out of shot. It was clear from the tilt and wobble of the frame that there was a degree of jostling going on. Vernon had a glimpse of the sky, then the cameraman's feet and orange tape. The whole circus must be there, confined behind a line. The picture found Mrs Garmony at last and steadied itself as she cleared her throat and prepared to make her statement. There was something in her hand, but she was not going to read from it because she was confident enough to speak without notes. She paused to ensure she had everyone's full attention, then began with a little history of her marriage, from the days when she was at the Guildhall dreaming of a career as a concert pianist, and Julian was an impoverished and high-spirited law student. Those were the days of hard work and making-do, the one-roomed flat in South London, the birth of Annabel, her own late decision to study medicine and Julian's unflinching support, the proud purchase of their first house at the less popular end of Fulham, the birth of Ned, Julian's growing success at the bar, her first internship, and so on. Her voice was relaxed, even intimate, and derived its authority not so much from class, or status as a Cabinet Minister's wife, as from her own professional eminence. She spoke of her pride in Julian's career, the delight they had taken in their children, how they had shared in each other's triumphs and setbacks and how they had always valued fun, discipline and, above all, honesty.

She paused and smiled, as though to herself. Right at the beginning, she said, Julian told her something about himself, something rather startling, even a little shocking. But it was nothing that their love could not absorb, and over the years it had endeared itself to her and she had come to regard it with respect, as an inseparable part of her husband's individuality. Their trust in each other had been absolute. It hadn't entirely been a secret either, this curious thing about Julian, because a friend of the family, Molly Lane who died recently, once took some pictures, rather in a spirit of celebration. Mrs Garmony was lifting up a white cardboard folder and as she did so Annabel kissed her father on the cheek, and Ned, who was now seen to be wearing a nose stud, leaned across and put a hand on his father's arm.

'Oh God,' Vernon croaked. 'It's a spoiler.'

She pulled the photographs clear and held up the first for all to see. It was the cat-walk pose, it was Vernon's front page. The camera wobbled as it zoomed in, and there was shouting and pushing behind the line. Mrs Garmony waited for the clamour to subside. When it had, she said calmly that she knew that a newspaper with a political agenda of its own intended to publish this photograph and others tomorrow in the expectation of driving her husband from office. She had only this to say: the newspaper would not succeed because love was a greater force than spite.

The line had broken and the hacks were surging forwards. Behind the five-barred gate the children had linked arms with their father, while their mother stood firm against the rabble, unfazed by the microphones shoved into her face. Vernon was out of his chair. No, Mrs Garmony was saying, and she was glad to be able to put the record straight and make it clear that there was absolutely no foundation in the rumour. Molly Lane was simply a family friend and the Garmonys would always remember her fondly. Vernon was on his way across his office to turn the thing off when the surgeon was asked whether she had any particular message for the editor of *The Judge*. Yes, she said, she did, and she looked at him, and he froze in front of the television.

'Mr Halliday, you have the mentality of a blackmailer, and the moral stature of a *flea*.'

Vernon gasped in pained admiration, for he knew a soundbite when he heard one. The question was a plant, the line was scripted. What consummate artistry!

She was about to say more, but he managed to lift a hand and switch off the set.

v

Around five o'clock that afternoon, it occurred to the
many newspaper editors who had bid for Molly's photographs that the trouble with Vernon's paper was that it
was out of step with changing times. As a leader in one
broadsheet put it to its readers on Friday morning: 'It
seems to have escaped the attention of the editor of *The
Judge* that the decade we live in now is not like the one
before. Then, self-advancement was the watchword, while
greed and hypocrisy were the rank realities. Now we live
in a more reasonable, compassionate and tolerant age in
which the private and harmless preferences of individuals,
however public they may be, remain their own business.
Where there is no discernible issue of public interest, the
old-fashioned arts of the blackmailer and self-righteous
whistle-blower have no place, and while this paper does
not wish to impugn the moral sensitivities of the common
flea, it cannot but endorse the remarks made yesterday
by . . .' etc.

Front-page headlines divided more or less equally
between 'blackmailer' and 'flea' and most made use of a
photograph of Vernon taken at a Press Association
banquet looking somewhat squiffy in a crumpled dinner
jacket. On Friday afternoon two thousand members of the
Transvestite Pink Alliance marched on Judge House in

their high heels, holding aloft copies of the disgraced front page and chanting in derisive falsetto. About the same time, the parliamentary party seized the moment and passed an overwhelming vote of confidence in the Foreign Secretary. The Prime Minister suddenly felt emboldened to speak up for his old friend. A broad consensus emerged over the weekend that *The Judge* had gone too far and was a disgusting newspaper, that Julian Garmony was a decent fellow and Vernon Halliday ('The Flea') was despicable and his head was urgently needed on a plate. In the Sundays, the lifestyle sections portrayed 'the new support-ive wife' who had her own career *and* fought her husband's corner. The editorials concentrated on the few remaining neglected aspects of Mrs Garmony's speech, including 'love is greater than spite'. On *The Judge* itself the senior staff were glad their reservations had been minuted, and it was felt by most journalists that Grant McDonald pointed the way when he was heard to say in the canteen that once his misgivings were not listened to, then he did his best to be loyal. By Monday they had all remembered their misgivings and how they had all tried to be loyal.

The matter was rather more complex for *The Judge*'s board of directors which met in emergency session on Monday afternoon. In fact, it was rather trying. How could they sack an editor to whom they had given a unanimous vote of support last Wednesday?

Finally, after two hours of meander and backtrack, George Lane had a good idea.

'Look, there was nothing wrong in purchasing those

photographs. Actually, I can tell you this, I heard he got a jolly good deal. No, Halliday's mistake was in not pulling his front page the moment he saw Rose Garmony's press conference. He had plenty of time to turn it around. He wasn't going out with it till the late edition. He was quite wrong to have gone ahead. On Friday the paper was made to look ridiculous. He should have seen which way the wind was blowing and got out. If you're asking me, it was a serious failure of editorial judgement.'

vi

The following day the editor presided over a subdued meeting with his senior staff. Tony Montano sat to one side, a silent observer.

'It's time we ran more regular columns. They're cheap, and everyone else is doing them. You know, we hire someone of low to medium intelligence, possibly female, to write about, well, nothing much. You've seen the sort of thing. Goes to a party and can't remember someone's name. Twelve hundred words.'

'Sort of navel gazing,' Jeremy Ball suggested.

'Not quite. Gazing is too intellectual. More like navel *chat*.'

'Can't work her video recorder. Is my bum too big?' Lettice supplied helpfully.

'That's good. Keep 'em coming.' The editor wiggled and paddled his fingers in the air to draw out their ideas.

'Er, buying a guinea pig.'

'His hangover.'

'Her first grey pubic hair.'

'Always gets the supermarket trolley with the wobbly wheel.'

'Excellent. I like it. Harvey? Grant?'

'Um, always losing Biros. Where do they go?'

'Ehm, canna keep his tongue out of the wee hole in his tooth.'

'Brilliant,' Frank said. 'Thank you, everyone. We'll continue this tomorrow.'

V

V

i

There were moments in the early morning, after the mild excitement of dawn, with London already heading noisily for work, and his creative turmoil finally smothered by exhaustion, when Clive stood from the piano and shuffled to the doorway to turn out the studio lights, and looked back at the rich, the beautiful chaos that surrounded his toils, and had once more a passing thought, the minuscule fragment of a suspicion that he would not have shared with a single person in the world, would not even have committed to his journal and whose key word he shaped in his mind only with reluctance; the thought was, quite simply, that it might not be going too far to say that he was . . . a genius. A genius. Though he sounded it guiltily on his inner ear, he would not let the word reach his lips. He was not a vain man. A genius. It was a term that had suffered from inflationary over-use, but surely there was a certain level of achievement, a gold standard, that was non-negotiable, beyond mere opinion. There hadn't been many. Among his countrymen, Shakespeare was a genius, of course, and Darwin and Newton, he had heard it said. Purcell, almost. Britten, less so, though within range. But there had been no Beethovens here.

When he had this suspicion about himself – and it had happened three or four times since he returned from the

Lake District – the world grew large and still, and in the grey-blue light of a March morning, his piano, the midi, the plates and cups, Molly's armchair, took on a sculpted, rounded appearance, reminding him of how things looked to him once in his youth when he took mescalin: bloated with volume, poised with benign significance. And he saw the studio he was about to abandon for his bed as it might have appeared in a documentary film about himself that would reveal to a curious world how a masterpiece was born. He also saw the grainy reverse, the figure lingering by the doorway in grubby loose white shirt, jeans roped in tight against a convexity of gut, eyes blackened and engorged by fatigue: the composer, heroic and endearing in his stubbly dishevelment. These were truly the great moments in a period of joyous creative outpouring such as he had never known, those moments when he stood from his work in a near-hallucinatory state, and floated down the stairs to his bedroom, kicked off his shoes and rolled under the covers to succumb to a dreamless sleep that was a sick numbness, a void, a death.

He woke in the late afternoon, pulled on his shoes and went down to the kitchen to eat the cold plate the housekeeper had left for him. He opened a bottle of wine and took it with him up to the studio where he would find a full coffee flask and would begin a new journey into the night. Somewhere at his back, stalking him like a beast and closing in, was the deadline. In just over a week he must confront Giulio Bo and the British Symphony Orchestra in Amsterdam for two days of rehearsal and, two days after that, the première in the Birmingham Free Trade Hall.

Given that the millennium's end was years away, the pressure was quite ridiculous. Already his fair copy of the first three movements had been taken away and the orchestral parts had been transcribed. His secretary had called a few times to collect the latest pages of the final movement, and a team of copyists was at work. For now there could be no backward glances and he could only push on and hope to be finished before next week. He complained, but in his heart he was untouched by the pressure, for this was how he needed to be working, lost to the mighty effort of bringing his work to its awesome finale. The ancient stone steps had been climbed, the wisps of sound had melted away like mist, his new melody, darkly scored in its first lonely manifestation for a muted trombone, had gathered around itself rich orchestral textures of sinuous harmony, then dissonance and whirling variations that spun away into space, never to reappear, and had now drawn itself up in a process of consolidation, like an explosion seen in reverse, funnelling inwards to a geometrical point of stillness; then the muted trombone again, and then, with a hushed crescendo, like a giant drawing breath, the final and colossal restatement of the melody (with one intriguing and as yet unsolved difference) which gathered pace, and erupted into a wave, a racing tsunami of sound reaching an impossible velocity, then rearing up, higher, and when it seemed beyond human capability, higher yet, and at last toppling, breaking and crashing vertiginously down to shatter on the hard safe ground of the home key of C minor. What remained were the pedal notes promising resolution and peace in infinite space. Then a diminuendo spanning forty-five seconds, dissolving into four bars of scored silence. The end.

And it was almost done. Wednesday night into Thursday morning Clive revised and perfected the diminuendo. All that was required now was go to back several pages in the score to the clamorous restatement and vary the harmonies perhaps, or even the melody itself, or devise some form of rhythmic undertow, a syncopation that cut into the leading edge of the notes. To Clive this variation had become a crucial feature of the work's conclusion; it needed to suggest the future's unknowability. When that by now familiar melody returned for the very last time, altered in a small and significant way, it should prompt insecurity in the listener; it was a caution against clinging too tightly to what we knew.

On Thursday morning he was in bed, thinking about this and falling asleep when Vernon phoned. The call was reassuring. Clive had been meaning to get in touch since he returned, but his work had swept him away, and Garmony, the photographs and *The Judge* seemed to him like sub-plots in a barely remembered movie. All he knew was that he did not wish to be quarrelling with anyone, least of all one of his oldest friends. When Vernon cut the conversation short and suggested coming by for a drink the following evening, it occurred to Clive that he might have finished by then. He would have written in that important change to the restatement, for it would surely take him no more than one all-night session. The last pages would have been taken away and he might ask in a few friends to make up a celebration party. These were his happy thoughts as he plunged into sleep. It was disorienting then to wake what seemed like two minutes later into Vernon's bullying interrogation.

'I want you to go to the police now and tell them what you saw.'

This was the sentence that jolted Clive into the truth. He emerged from a tunnel into clarity. In fact, what came back to him was the train journey to Penrith, and those half-forgotten insights, and their sour taste. Each exchange was a click on the ratchet -- no slipping back into civility. By invoking Molly's memory -- 'meaning crapping on Molly's grave' -- Clive allowed a full flood of hot indignation to bathe him, and when Vernon outrageously threatened to go to the police himself, Clive gasped and kicked the bedclothes clear and stood in his socks by the bedside table for the concluding barter of abuse. Vernon hung up on him, just as he was about to hang up on Vernon. Without bothering to lace up his shoes, Clive ran down the stairs in a fury, cursing as he went. It wasn't yet five o'clock, but he was having a drink, he deserved a drink and he'd punch the man who tried to stop him. But he was alone, of course, and thank God. It was a gin and tonic, though mostly it was a gin, and he stood by the draining board and sank it, without ice or lemon, and thought bitterly of the outrage. The *outrage* of it! He was framing the letter he would like to send to this scum he mistook for a friend. Him, with his loathsome daily round, his sordid cynical scheming mind, the wheedling sponging hypocritical passive-aggressive. Vermin Halliday, who knew nothing of what it was to create, because he'd never made anything good in his life, and was eaten up with hatred for those who could. His poky suburban squeamishness was what passed for a moral stand, and meanwhile he was up to the elbows in shit, in fact he had verily pitched his tent on excrement, and to advance his squalid interests he was happy to debase Molly's memory and ruin a vulnerable fool like Garmony and call up the hate codes of the yellow press and all along pretend to himself, and tell anyone who would listen – and this was what took the breath away – that he was doing his duty, that he was in the service of some high ideal. He was mad, he was sick, he didn't deserve to exist!

These kitchen execrations saw Clive through a second drink, and then a third. He knew from long experience that a letter sent in fury merely put a weapon into the hands of your enemy. Poison, in preserved form, to be used against you long into the future. But Clive wanted to write something now precisely because he might not feel so strongly in a week's time. He compromised with a terse postcard which he would leave for a day before sending. *Your threat appals me. So does your journalism. You deserve to be sacked. Clive.* He opened a bottle of Chablis and, ignoring the saumon en croute in the fridge, went up to the top floor, belligerently determined to start work. There would come a time when nothing would remain of Vermin Halliday, but what would remain of Clive Linley would be his music. Work, quiet, determined, triumphant work then, would be a kind of revenge. But belligerence was a poor aid to concentration, as were three gins and a bottle of wine, and three hours later he was still staring at the score on the piano, in a hunched attitude of work, with a pencil in his hand and a frown, but hearing and seeing only the bright hurdy-gurdy carousel of his twirling thoughts, and the same hard little horses bobbing by on their braided rods. Here they came again. The outrage! The police! Poor Molly! Sanctimonious bastard! Call that a moral position? Up to his neck in shit! The *outrage*! And what about Molly . . . ?

At nine thirty he stood and decided to pull himself together, drink some red wine and get on with the work. There was his beautiful theme, his song, spread out on the page, craving his attention, needing one inspired modification, and here he was, alive with focused energy, ready to make it. But downstairs he lingered in the kitchen over his rediscovered supper, listening to a history of the nomadic Moroccan Tuareg people on the radio, and then he took his third glass of Bandol for a wander about the house, an anthropologist to his own existence. He hadn't been in the living room for over a week and now he drifted about the enormous room, examining paintings and photographs as though for the first time, running a hand over the furniture and picking up objects from above the mantelpiece. His whole life was in here, and what a rich history! The money to buy even the cheapest of these things had been earned by Clive dreaming up sounds, by putting one note in front of another. He had imagined everything here, he had willed it all to be here, without anyone's help. And he drank to his success, down in one, and returned to the kitchen for a refill before setting out for a tour of the dining room. At eleven thirty he was back in front of the score whose notes now would not hold still, not even for him, and he had to agree with himself that he was seriously drunk, and who wouldn't be after such betrayals? There was a half bottle of Scotch on a bookcase which he took to Molly's chair and there was some Ravel already in the machine. His last memory of the evening was of lifting the remote control and pointing at the disc player.

He woke in the small hours with the headphones askew across his face and a terrible thirst from dreams of crossing a desert on hands and knees, carrying the Tuaregs' only grand piano. He drank from the bathroom tap and put himself to bed, and lay there for hours, open-eyed in the dark, exhausted, desiccated and alert, once more forced to attend helplessly to his carousel. *Neck in shit? Moral position! Molly?*

When he woke from a brief sleep in the mid morning, he knew the roll, the creative spree, was over. It was not simply that he was tired and hung-over. As soon as he sat at the piano and tried out a couple of approaches to the variation, he found that not only this passage, but the whole movement had died on him – suddenly it was ashes in his mouth. He didn't dare think too hard about the symphony itself. When his secretary called to try to make arrangements for collecting the final pages, he was short with her and had to phone back with an apology. He took a walk to clear his head, and post the card to Vernon which today read like a masterpiece of restraint. Along the way he bought a copy of *The Judge*; to protect his concentration he had been denying himself newspapers, or the TV and radio news, so he had missed the build-up.

It was a shock, then, at home, when he spread out the paper on the kitchen table. Garmony posing before Molly, camping it up for her, and the camera in her warm hands, her living eye once framing what Clive saw now. But the front page was an embarrassment, not because, or not only because, a man had been caught out in a delicate private moment, but because the paper had worked itself up into such a lather about it and brought to bear such powerful resources. As if some criminal political conspiracy had been uncovered, or a corpse under the table in the Foreign Office. So unworldly, so misjudged, so uncool. It was inept too in the ways it tried so hard to be cruel. The overstated and contemptuous cartoon, for example, and the crowing leader with its childish pun on 'drag', the doomed crowd-pleaser of 'knickers in a twist', and the feebly opposed 'dressing up' and 'dressing down'. Again the thought recurred: not only was Vernon loathsome, he had to be mad. But that wouldn't stop Clive loathing him.

The hangover lasted all weekend and into Monday – one didn't get off so lightly these days – and the general nausea presented an appropriate background for bitter brooding. The work was stalled. What had been a luscious fruit was now a dry twig. The copyists were desperate to receive the last twelve pages of the score. The orchestra manager phoned three times, his voice trembling in controlled panic. The Concertgebouw had been booked from next Friday for two days' rehearsal at huge expense, the extra percussionists Clive had asked for had been retained, along with the accordionist. Giulio Bo was impatient to have sight of the work's conclusion, and all the arrangements had been made for Birmingham. If there was no complete parts score in Amsterdam by Thursday he – the manager – would have no option but to drown himself in the nearest canal. It was soothing to be exposed to an anguish greater than his own, but still Clive refused to let the pages go. He was holding out for his significant variation and, in the way of these things, it was beginning to seem to him that the work's integrity depended on it.

This, of course, was a ruinous conception. When he entered the studio now its squalor oppressed him, and when he sat in front of his manuscript – the handwriting of a younger, more confident and gifted man – he blamed Vernon for the fact that he could not work, and his anger redoubled. His concentration had been shattered. By an idiot. It was becoming clear that he had been denied his masterpiece, the summit of a lifetime's work. This symphony would have taught his audience how to listen to, how to *hear*, everything else he had ever written. Now the proof, the very signature, of genius had been spoiled, and greatness had been snatched away. For Clive knew that he would never again attempt a composition on such a scale; he was too weary, too emptied out, too old. On Sunday he lolled about the sitting room numbly reading the rest of the stories in Friday's *Judge*. The world was its usual mess: fish were changing sex, British table tennis had lost its way, and in Holland some unsavoury types with medical degrees were offering a legal service to eliminate your inconvenient elderly parent. How interesting. All one needed was the aged parent's signature in duplicate and several thousand dollars. In the afternoon he took a long walk around Hyde Park and reflected at length on this article. It was true, he had entered into an agreement with Vernon which, after all, entailed certain obligations. Perhaps a little research was in order. But Monday was wasted in a pretence of work, a self-deceiving tinkering that he had the sense to abandon in the evening. Every idea he had was dull. He shouldn't be let near this symphony; he was not worthy of his own creation.

On Tuesday morning he was woken by the orchestral manager who actually shouted at him down the phone. Rehearsals on Friday, and still they had no complete score. Later the same morning Clive heard on the phone from a friend the extraordinary news. Vernon had been forced to resign! Clive hurried out to buy the papers. He had read or heard nothing since Friday's *Judge*, otherwise he would have been aware of how opinion had been turning against its editor. He took a cup of coffee into the dining room and read the press there. It was grimly satisfying to have his own views of Vernon's conduct confirmed. He had done his duty by Vernon, he tried to warn him, but Vernon wouldn't listen. Having read three scathing indictments, Clive went to the window and stared at the clumps of daffodils growing by the apple tree at the bottom of the garden. He had to admit it, he was feeling better. Early spring. Soon the clocks would go forwards. In April, with the symphony's première behind him, he'd go to New York to visit Susie Marcellan. Then to California where he had a piece in the Palo Alto Music Festival. He was aware that his finger was tapping the radiator to the beat of some new rhythm, and he imagined a shift of mood, of key, and a note sustained over changing harmonies and a savage kettle-drum pulse. He turned and hurried from the room. He had an idea, a quarter of an idea, and before it went he had to get to the piano.

In the studio he shoved books and old scores to the floor to make himself a clear surface, took up a sheet of lined paper and a sharpened pencil, and had just formed a treble clef when the doorbell downstairs rang. His hand froze, and he waited. It rang again. He was not going down, not now, when he was about to crack the variation. It would be someone pretending to be an ex-coal miner in order to sell ironing-board covers. The bell again, then silence. They'd gone. For a moment, the slender idea he had was lost. Then he had it, or part of it, and was just drawing the stem of a chord when the phone rang. He should have turned it off. In his irritation, he snatched it up.

'Mr Linley?'

'Yes.'

'Police. C.I.D. Standing outside your front door. Appreciate a word.'

'Oh. Look, can you come back in half an hour?'

''Fraid not. Got a few questions for you. Might have to ask you to attend a couple of identity parades in Manchester. Help us nail a suspect. Shouldn't take up more than a couple of days of your time. So, if you wouldn't mind opening up, Mr Linley . . .'

ii

In her hurry to get off to work, Mandy had left a wardrobe door open at an angle that allowed a mirror to accuse Vernon with a narrow, vertical slice of himself: propped against the pillows, resting the mug of tea she had brought him against his belly, his unshaved face bluish-white in the bedroom gloom, letters, junk mail and newspapers spread beside him – truly, a tableau of unemployment. *Idle*. Suddenly he understood that business-page word. He had many idle hours ahead of him this Tuesday morning to brood on all the indignities and ironies that had accumulated about his dismissal yesterday. The curious way, for example, the letter was dropped off in his office by an innocent sub, that very same sobbing dyslexic sub he had saved from the push. Then the letter itself, politely soliciting his resignation and offering in return a year's salary. There was a muted reference to the terms of his contract, by which, he assumed, the directors wished to remind him, without spelling it out, that if he refused, and forced them to sack him, there would be no remuneration at all. The letter concluded by observing kindly that, in any event, his employment would cease that day and that the board wished to congratulate him on his period of brilliant editorship, and to wish him well in his future plans. So there it was. He had to clear out now, and he could leave with or without a sum in the low six figures.

In his resignation letter Vernon had noted that circulation was up by more than a hundred thousand. Just writing out the number, the zeros, pained him. When he went to the outer office and handed the envelope to Jean, she seemed to have difficulty looking him in the eye. And the building was curiously silent as he returned to collect his things from his desk. His office instincts told him that everybody knew. He left his door open in case anyone felt like coming by in the way of fellow feeling, down the beaten track of friendship. What there was to pack easily fitted into his briefcase – a framed photograph of Mandy and the kids, a couple of pornographic letters from Dana, written on House of Commons paper. And it looked like no one was popping in to express their outraged sympathy. No raucous crowd of shirt-sleeved colleagues to bang him out in the old style. Very well then, he was leaving. He buzzed Jean and asked her to let the chauffeur know he was coming down. She buzzed back to tell him he no longer had a chauffeur.

He put on his coat, picked up his briefcase and went into the outer office. Jean had found herself an urgent errand, and he met no one, not a soul, on his way to the lift. The only person to say cheerio to the editor was the porter downstairs on the desk, and he was also the one to inform Vernon of his successor. Mr Dibben, sir. By minimally inclining his head, Vernon managed to convey the pretence that he already knew. When he stepped outside Judge House, it was raining. He raised an arm for a taxi, then remembered that he had very little cash with him. He took the tube, and walked the last half mile to his home in a downpour. He went straight for the whisky, and when Mandy came in he had a terrible row with her, when all she was trying to do was comfort him.

Vernon slumped with his tea while his mental odometer tallied the insults and humiliations. Not enough that Frank Dibben was treacherous, that all his colleagues deserted him, that every newspaper was cheering his dismissal; not enough that the whole country celebrated the crushing of the flea, and that Garmony was still at large. Lying on the bed beside him was a venomous little card gloating over his downfall, written by his oldest friend, written by a man so morally eminent he would rather see a woman raped in front of him than have his work disrupted. Perfectly hateful, and mad. Vindictive. So it was war. Right then. Here we go, don't hesitate. He drained his cup, picked up the phone and dialled a friend at New Scotland Yard, a contact from his old crime-desk days. Fifteen minutes later all the details had been imparted, the deed was done, but Vernon was still back with his thoughts, still not satisfied. It turned out that Clive had not broken the law. He would be inconvenienced into doing his duty, nothing more than that. But there had to be more. There had to be consequences. Vernon brooded another hour in bed on this theme, then at last got dressed, though he did not shave, and passed the morning moping about the house, refusing to answer the phone. For consolation he took out the Friday edition. The fact was, it was a brilliant front page. Everyone was wrong. The rest of the paper was strong too, and Lettice O'Hara had done him proud with the Dutch story. One day, especially if Garmony ever got to be Prime Minister and the country was lying in ruins, people would regret they had hounded Vernon Halliday from his job.

But the consolation was brief because that was the future, and this was the present, the one in which he had been sacked. He was at home when he should have been in an office. He knew only one profession and no one would employ him in it now. He was in disgrace and he was too old to retrain. His consolation was also brief because his thoughts kept returning to that hateful postcard, the twisting knife, the salt in his lacerations, and as the day passed it came to stand for all the major and minor insults of the past twenty-four hours. That little message to him from Clive embodied and condensed all the poison of this affair – the blindness of his accusers, their hypocrisy, their vengefulness, and above all the element that Vernon considered to be the worst of human vices – personal betrayal.

In a language as idiomatically stressed as English, opportunities for misreadings are bound to arise. By a mere backward movement of stress, a verb can become a noun, an act a thing. To refuse – to insist on saying no to what you believe is wrong – becomes at a stroke, refuse – an insurmountable pile of garbage. As with words, so with sentences. What Clive had intended on Thursday and posted on Friday was, You deserve to be *sacked*. What Vernon was bound to understand on Tuesday in the aftermath of his dismissal was, You *deserve* to be sacked. Had the card arrived on Monday, he might have read it differently. This was the comic nature of their fate; a first-class stamp would have served both men well. On the other hand, perhaps no other outcomes were available to them, and this was the nature of their tragedy. If so, Vernon was bound to consolidate his bitterness as the day wore on and reflect, rather opportunistically, on the pact the two men had made not so long ago and the awesome responsibilities it laid upon him. For clearly, Clive had lost his reason and something had to be done. This resolve was bolstered by Vernon's sense that, at a time when the world was treating him badly, when his life was in ruins, no one was treating him worse than his old friend, and that this was unforgivable. And insane. It can happen sometimes with those who brood on an injustice, that a taste for revenge can usefully combine with a sense of obligation. The hours passed, and Vernon picked up his copy of *The Judge* several times to read again about the medical scandal in Holland. Later on in the day he made a few phone enquiries of his own. More idle hours passed while he sat about in the kitchen drinking coffee, contemplating the wreck of his prospects, and wondering whether he should ring Clive and pretend to make peace, in order to invite himself to Amsterdam.

Was everything in place? Had he remembered everything? Was it really legal? Clive considered these questions from the confines of a Boeing 757 parked in freezing fog at the northern end of Manchester airport. The weather was supposed to clear and the pilot wanted to keep his place in the take-off queue, so the passengers sat in muffled silence taking comfort in the drinks trolley. It was midday and Clive had ordered coffee, brandy and a bar of chocolate. He had a window seat in an empty row, and through gaps in the fog he could see other airliners waiting competitively in ragged, converging lines, something brooding and loutish in their forms: slit eyes beneath small brains, stunted, encumbered arms, upraised and blackened arse-holes – creatures like this could never care about each other.

The answer was yes, his research and planning had been meticulous. It was going to happen, and he experienced a thrill. He raised his hand to the smiling girl in a cocky blue hat who seemed personally delighted by his decision to go for the second miniature, and privileged to bring it to him. All in all, given what he'd been through and the ordeals that lay ahead, and the certainty that events now were sure to accelerate giddily, he didn't feel so bad. He would miss the first hours of rehearsal, but an orchestra finding its way through a new piece – always a dog's dinner. It might be sensible to miss the whole of the first day. He had been reassured by his bank that to have ten thousand US dollars in his briefcase was within the law and he was not required to explain himself at Schiphol airport. As for Manchester police station, he had handled it capably, he thought, and was treated with respect, and he could almost feel a touch of nostalgia for the bracing ambience and those hard-pressed men with whom he had worked so well.

When Clive arrived from the railway station in the blackest of moods, having cursed Vernon every mile of the way from Euston, the Chief Inspector himself came out to the front desk to welcome the great composer. He seemed awfully grateful that Clive should have come all the way up from London to help with the case. In fact, no one seemed at all annoyed that he hadn't come forward earlier. They were only too happy, various policemen said, to have his assistance with this particular crime. In interview, when he made his statement, the two detectives realised, so they assured him, just how hard it must have been to write a symphony to order with a looming deadline, and what a dilemma he had been in when he was crouching behind that rock. They seemed rather keen to understand all the difficulties associated with composing the crucial melody. Could he hum it for them? He certainly could. Every now and then one of them would say something like, Now just take us back to what you saw of this man. It turned out that the Chief Inspector was working for an English degree at the Open University and had a special interest in Blake. In the canteen, over bacon sandwiches, the Inspector proved he knew by heart the whole of 'A Poison Tree', and Clive was able to tell him of his 1978 setting of that very same poem, performed at the Aldeburgh Festival the next year with Peter Pears, and never once since. Also in the canteen, lying asleep on two chairs pushed together, was a six-month-old baby. The young mother was locked up in a cell on the ground floor while she recovered from a drinking binge. Throughout the first day Clive sometimes heard her plaintive shrieks and moans drifting up the peeling stairwell.

He was allowed to come through to the heart of the station, where people were charged. In the early evening, while he was waiting to go over his statement again, he witnessed a scuffle in front of the duty sergeant; a big, sweating teenager with a shaved head had been picked up hiding in a back garden with bolt cutters, master keys, padsaw and a sledgehammer concealed beneath his coat. He was not a burglar, he insisted, and no way was he going in the cells. When the sergeant told him he was, the boy hit a constable in the face and was wrestled to the floor by two other constables who put handcuffs on him and led him away. No one seemed much bothered, not even the policeman with the split lip, but Clive put a restraining hand over his leaping heart and was obliged to sit down. Later, a patrolman carried in a white-faced, silent four-year-old boy who had been found wandering about the car park of a derelict pub. Later still, a tearful Irish family came to claim him. Two hair-chewing girls, twin daughters of a violent father, came in for their own protection and were treated with jokey familiarity. A woman with a bleeding face lodged a complaint against her husband. A very ancient black lady whom osteoporosis had folded double had been thrown out of her room by her daughter-in-law and had nowhere to go. Social workers came and went and most of them looked as criminally inclined, or as unfortunate, as their clients. Everybody smoked. In the fluorescent light everybody looked ill. There was a lot of scorching tea in plastic cups, and there was a lot of shouting, and routine, uncolourful swearing, and clenched-fist threats that no one took seriously. It was one huge unhappy family with domestic problems that were of their nature insoluble. This was the family living room. Clive shrank behind his brick-red tea. In his world it was rare for someone to raise his voice, and he found himself all evening in a state of exhausted excitement. Practically every member of the public who came in, voluntarily or not, was down at heel, and it seemed to Clive that the main business of the police was to deal with the numerous and unpredictable consequences of poverty, which they did with far more patience and less squeamishness than he ever could.

To think, he had once called them pigs and argued, during a three-month flirtation with anarchism in 1967, that they were the cause of crime, and would one day be unnecessary. The whole time he was there he was treated with courtesy and even deference. They seemed to *like* him, these policemen, and Clive wondered if there were not certain qualities he never knew he possessed – a level manner, quiet charm, authority perhaps. By the time it came to the identity parade early the following morning, he was anxious not to let anyone down. He was led out into a yard behind where the patrol cars parked, and there were a dozen men standing by a wall. Straight away he saw his man, third from the right, the one with the long thin face and the tell-tale cloth cap. What a relief. When they went back inside one of the detectives gripped Clive's arm and squeezed, but said nothing. Around him was an atmosphere of suppressed rejoicing and everyone liked him even more. They were working together as a team now and Clive had accepted his role as a key prosecution witness. Later on there was a second parade and this time half the men had cloth caps and all had long thin faces. But Clive wasn't fooled and found his man right at the end, without a cap. Back indoors he was told by the detectives that this second line-up was not so important. In fact, for administrative reasons they might even discount it completely. Generally though, they were delighted with his commitment to the cause. Consider himself an honorary policeman. They had a patrol car going out towards the airport. Would he like a lift in that direction?

He was dropped right by the terminal building. As he was getting out of the back seat and saying his goodbyes, he noticed that the policeman in the driver's seat was the very man he had picked out of the line the second time. But neither Clive nor the driver found it necessary to comment on the fact as they shook hands.

iv

The flight was two hours late into Schiphol airport. Clive took the train to the Central Station and from there set off on foot for his hotel in the soft grey afternoon light. While he was crossing the Bridge it came back to him, what a calm and civilised city Amsterdam was. He took a wide detour westwards in order to stroll along Brouwersgracht. His suitcase, after all, was very light. So consoling, to have a body of water down the middle of a street. Such a tolerant, open-minded, grown-up sort of place: the beautiful brick and carved timber warehouses converted into tasteful apartments, the modest Van Gogh bridges, the understated street furniture, the intelligent, unstuffy-looking Dutch on their bikes with their level-headed children sitting behind. Even the shopkeepers looked like professors, the street sweepers like jazz musicians. There was never a city more rationally ordered. As he walked along, he thought about Vernon, and the symphony. Was the work ruined, or simply flawed? Perhaps not flawed so much as sullied, and in ways that only he could understand. Ruinously cheated of its greatest moment. He dreaded the première. He could tell himself now, in all tortuous sincerity, that in making his various arrangements on Vernon's behalf he, Clive, was doing no more than honouring his word. That Vernon should want a reconciliation and should therefore want to come to Amsterdam was surely more than a coincidence, or a neat convenience. Somewhere in his blackened, unbalanced heart he had accepted his fate. He was delivering himself up to Clive.

These reflections brought Clive at last to his hotel where he learned that the reception tonight would be at seven thirty. From his room he called his contact, the good doctor, to discuss arrangements and, for one last time, the symptoms: unpredictable, bizarre and extreme antisocial behaviour, a complete loss of reason. Destructive tendencies, delusions of omnipotence. A disintegrated personality. The matter of pre-medication was discussed. How should it be administered? A glass of champagne was suggested, which seemed to Clive to strike the appropriate festive note.

There were still two hours of rehearsal, so, having left the money in an envelope at reception, Clive had the doorman wave down a taxi for him outside the hotel, and within a few minutes was at the artists' entrance round the side of the Concertgebouw. As he passed the porter and pushed open the swing doors that led to the stairs, the sound of the orchestra reached him. The final movement. It was bound to be. As he went up he was already correcting the passage; it was the French horns we should have been hearing now, not the clarinets, and the timpani markings were piano. *This is my music.* It was as though hunting horns were calling him, calling him back to himself. How could he have forgotten? He quickened his stride. He could hear what he had written. He was walking towards a representation of himself. All those nights alone.

The hateful press. Allen Crags. Why had he been wasting time all afternoon, why had he been delaying the moment? It was an effort to stop himself running down the curving corridor that led around the auditorium. He pushed open a door and paused.

He had arrived, as he had intended, in the stalls above and behind the orchestra, behind the percussionists in fact. The musicians could not see him, but he was right in view of the conductor. Giulio Bo's eyes, however, were closed. He was standing on tiptoes, craning forwards, his left arm extended towards the orchestra and with splayed, trembling fingers was gently lifting into being the muted trombone that now delivered, sweetly, wisely, conspiratorially, the first full statement of the melody, the 'Nessun dorma' of the century's end, the melody Clive had hummed to the detectives yesterday and for which he was prepared to sacrifice an anonymous rambler. And rightly. As the notes swelled, as the whole string section positioned their bows to breathe the first sustaining whispers of their sinuous sliding harmonies, Clive slipped quietly into a seat and felt himself tumbling into a kind of swoon. Now the textures were multiplying as more instruments were drawn into the trombone's conspiracy, and dissonance was spreading like a contagion, and little hard splinters – the variations that would lead nowhere – were tossed up like sparks which sometimes collided to produce the earliest intimations of the racing wall of sound, the tsunami, that now began to rise up and soon would obliterate everything in its path, before destroying itself on the bedrock of the tonic key. But before this could happen the conductor rapped his baton on his desk, and the orchestra raggedly and reluctantly subsided. Bo waited for the very last instrument to fall silent, then he lifted both hands in Clive's direction, and called.

'Maestro, welcome!'

The head of every member of the British Symphony Orchestra turned as Clive got to his feet. As he descended to the stage there was a clatter of bows against music stands. A trumpet sounded a witty four-note quotation from the D major concerto, Clive's, not Haydn's. Ah, to be in continental Europe and be maestro! What balm. He embraced Giulio, shook the hand of the leader, acknowledged the musicians with a smile, a little bow and hands half raised in modest surrender, then turned back to the conductor to murmur in his ear. Clive wouldn't address the orchestra today about the piece. He would do it in the morning, when everyone was fresh. For the moment he was happy to sit back and listen. He added his note about the clarinet and French horns, and the timpani's piano.

'Yes, yes,' Giulio said quickly. 'I've seen it.'

As Clive returned to his seat he noticed how solemn the faces of the musicians were. They had been working hard all day. The reception at the hotel would surely lift their spirits. The rehearsal continued, with Bo refining the passage he had just heard, listening to different sections of the orchestra independently and asking for adjustments in, among other things, the legato markings. From where he sat, Clive tried to prevent his attention being drawn into technical detail. For now, it was the music, the wondrous transformation of thought into sound. He hunched forwards, eyes closed, concentrating on each fragment that Bo permitted. Sometimes Clive worked so hard on a piece that he could lose sight of his ultimate purpose – to create this pleasure at once so sensual and abstract, to translate into vibrating air this non-language whose meanings were forever just beyond reach, suspended tantalisingly at a point where emotion and intellect fused. Certain sequences of notes reminded him of nothing more than the recent effort to write them. Bo was now working on the next passage, not quite a diminuendo so much as a shrinking away, and the music conjured for Clive the disorder of his studio in the dawn light, and the suspicions he had had about himself and hardly dared frame. Greatness. Was he an idiot to have thought this way? Surely there had to be one first single moment of self-recognition, and surely it would always seem absurd.

Now it was the trombone again and a tangled, half-suppressed crescendo that erupted at last into the melody's final statement, a blaring, carnivalesque tutti. *But fatally unvaried.* Clive put his face into his hands. He was right to have worried. It was ruined goods. Before he left for Manchester he had let the pages go as they were. There was no choice. Now he could not remember the exquisite change he had been about to make. This should have been the symphony's moment of triumphant assertion, the gathering up of all that was joyously human before the destruction to come. But presented like this, as a simple fortissimo repetition, it was literal-minded bombast, it was bathos; less than that, it was a void; one that only revenge could fill.

Because rehearsal time was running out, Bo let the orchestra play on to the end. Clive slumped in his seat. It all sounded different to him now. The theme was disintegrating into the tidal wave of dissonance and was gathering in volume – but it sounded quite absurd, like twenty orchestras tuning to an A. It was not dissonant at all. Practically every instrument was playing the same note. It was a drone. It was a giant bagpipe in need of repair. He could only hear the A, tossed from one instrument, one section, to another. Suddenly Clive's gift of perfect pitch was an affliction. That A was drilling through his head. He wanted to run from the auditorium, but he was right in Giulio's sight-line, and the repercussions of leaving his own rehearsal minutes before the end were unthinkable. So he slumped further into his seat and buried his face in an attitude of profound concentration and suffered right through to the final four-bar silence.

It was agreed that Clive would travel back to the hotel in the conductor's Rolls which was waiting by the artists' entrance. But Bo was caught up in orchestra business, so Clive had a few minutes to himself in the darkness outside the Concertgebouw. He walked through the crowds on Van Baerlestraat. People were already beginning to arrive for the evening's concert. Schubert. (Hadn't the world heard enough from syphilitic Schubert?) He stood on a street corner and breathed the mild Amsterdam air that always seemed to taste faintly of cigar smoke and ketchup. He knew his own score well enough, and how many A's were there and how that section really sounded. He had just experienced an auditory hallucination, an illusion – or a dis-illusion. The absence of the variation had wrecked his masterpiece, and he was clearer than ever now, if such a thing was possible, about the plans he had made. It was no longer fury that drove him, or hatred or disgust, or the necessity of honouring his word. What he was about to do was contractually right, it had the amoral inevitability of pure geometry, and he didn't feel a thing.

In the car Bo took him through the day's work, the many sections that seemed to play straight from the page, and the one or two that would have to be picked apart tomorrow. Despite his awareness of its imperfections, Clive wanted the great conductor to bless his symphony with a lofty compliment and angled a question accordingly:

'Do you think the whole piece is hanging together well? Structurally, I mean.'

Giulio leaned forward to slide shut the glass that separated them from his chauffeur.

'Is fine, everything is fine. But between you and me . . .' He lowered his voice. 'I think the second oboe, the young girl, is very beautiful but the playing is not perfect. Fortunately you have written nothing difficult for her. Very beautiful. Tonight she will have dinner with me.'

For the rest of the short journey Bo reminisced about the BSO's European tour which was almost at an end, and Clive recalled the last occasion the two of them worked together, in Prague on a revival of the *Symphonic Dervishes*.

'Ah yes,' Bo exclaimed as the car stopped outside the hotel and the door was held open for him. 'I remember it. A magnificent piece of work! The inventiveness of youth, so hard to recapture, eh Maestro?'

They parted company in the lobby, Bo to make a quick appearance at the reception, Clive to collect an envelope from the desk. He was informed that Vernon had arrived half an hour ago and had gone to a meeting. The drinks party for orchestra, friends and press was being held in a long chandeliered gallery at the rear of the hotel. A waiter was standing by the door with a tray from which Clive took a glass for Vernon and one for himself, then retreated to a deserted corner where he settled on a cushioned window seat to read the doctor's instructions and open a sachet of white powder. From time to time he glanced towards the door. When Vernon had phoned earlier in the week to apologise for setting on the police – I was an idiot, pressure of work, nightmare week, and so on – and especially when he proposed coming to Amsterdam to seal the reconciliation, saying he had business there anyway, Clive had been plausibly gracious in reply, but his hands were shaking when he put down the phone. They were shaking now as he tipped the powder into Vernon's champagne which effervesced briefly, then subsided. With his little finger Clive wiped away the greyish scum that had collected round the rim of the glass. Then he stood and took a glass in each hand. Vernon's in the right, his own in the left. Important to remember that. Vernon was right. Even though he was wrong.

Only one problem now preoccupied Clive as he made

his way through the cocktail roar of musicians, arts administrators and critics: how to persuade Vernon to take this drink before the doctor came. To take this drink rather than another. Best, perhaps, to intercept him by the door, before he reached for one from the tray. Champagne slopped over his wrists as he edged round the loud brass section, and he had to go a long way back up the gallery to avoid getting close to the basses who already seemed drunk, in competition with the timpani. At last he attained the tempered sodality of the violins who had permitted flutes and piccolo to join them. There were more women here to exert a tranquillising effect. They stood about in softly trilling duets and trios, and the air was pleasantly heavy with their perfume. To one side three men were discussing Flaubert in whispers. Clive found a unoccupied patch of carpet from where he had a clear view of the high double doors that gave on to the lobby. Sooner or later someone was going to come and talk to him. Sooner. It was that little shit Paul Lanark, the critic who had pronounced Clive the thinking man's Gorecki, then later publicly recanted: Gorecki was the thinking man's Linley. It was a wonder he had the nerve to approach.

'Ah, Linley. Is one of those for me?'

'No. And kindly bugger off.'

He would have been happy to give Lanark the drink in his right hand. Clive half turned away, but the critic was drunk and looking to have fun.

'I've been hearing about your latest. Is it really called the *Millennial Symphony*?'

'No. The press called it that,' Clive said stiffly.

'I've been hearing all about it. They say you've ripped off Beethoven something rotten.'

'Go away.'

'I suppose you'd call it sampling. Or post-modern quotation. But aren't you meant to be pre-modern?'

'If you don't go away I shall smack your stupid face.'

'Then you'd better give me one of those to free up a hand.'

As Clive was looking round for somewhere to put down the drinks, he saw Vernon coming towards him with a big smile. Unfortunately, he had two full glasses of his own.

'Clive!'

'Vernon!'

'Ah.' Lanark mimicked adulation. 'The Flea itself.'

'Look,' Clive said. 'I had a drink all ready for you.'

'And I got one for you.'

'Well . . .'

They each presented a glass to Lanark. Then Vernon offered a glass to Clive, and Clive gave his to Vernon.

'Cheers!'

Vernon gave Clive a nod and a meaningful look, and then turned to Lanark.

'I recently saw your name on a list of some very distinguished people. Judges, chief constables, top business people, government ministers . . .'

Lanark flushed with pleasure. 'All this stuff about a knighthood is complete nonsense.'

'It's certain to be. This concerns a children's home in Wales. Top notch paedophile ring. You were videoed going in and out half a dozen times. We were thinking of running a piece before I got bounced, but I'm sure someone else will pick it up.'

For at least ten seconds Lanark stood erect and motionless, with military dignity, elbows tucked in at his sides, champagnes held out before him, and a remote grin frozen on his lips. The warning signs were a certain bulge and glaze in the eye, and an upward rippling movement in his throat, a reverse peristalsis.

'Watch out!' Vernon cried. 'Get back!' They just managed to leap clear of the arced contents of Lanark's stomach. The gallery was suddenly silent. Then, with an extended, falling glissando of disgust, the whole string section, plus flutes and piccolo, surged towards the brass, leaving the music critic and his deed – an early-evening frites and mayonnaise on Oude Hoogstraat – illuminated under a lonely chandelier. Clive and Vernon were borne away with the crowd, and as they drew level with the door were able to extricate themselves and step into the calm of the lobby. They settled themselves on a banquette and continued sipping their champagne. 'Better than hitting him,' Clive said. 'Was any of it true?'

'I didn't used to think so.'

'Cheers again.'

'Cheers. And look, I meant what I said. I really am sorry about sending the police round to you. It was appalling behaviour. Unconditional, grovelling apologies.'

'Don't mention it again. I'm terribly sorry about your job and all that business. You really were the best.'

'Let's shake on it then. Friends.'

'Friends.'

Vernon emptied his glass, yawned and stood. 'Well look, if we're having supper together I might take a short nap. I'm feeling quite whacked.'

'You've had a heavy week. I think I'll take a bath. See you down here in about an hour?'

'Fine.'

Clive watched Vernon slouch away to collect his key from the desk. Standing at the foot of the grand double staircase were a man and a woman who met Clive's gaze and nodded. A moment later they followed Vernon up the stairs and Clive took a couple of turns around the lobby. Then he collected his own key and went to his room.

Minutes later he was standing in the bathroom barefoot, but otherwise fully clothed, bending over the tub, trying to manipulate the shimmering gold-plated mechanism that stopped the plughole. It needed to be simultaneously lifted and turned, and he didn't seem to have the knack. Meanwhile, the heated marble floor was communicating through the soles of his feet a reminder of sensuous fatigue. White nights in South Ken, mayhem in the police station, accolades in the Concertgebouw; he'd had a heavy week too. A short nap then before his bath. Back in the bedroom he floated free of his trousers, loosened his shirt and with a moan of pleasure abandoned himself to the giant bed. The gold satin bedspread caressed his thighs and he experienced an ecstasy of exhausted surrender. Everything was well. Soon he would be in New York to see Susie Marcellan, and that forgotten, buttoned-down part of him would flourish again. Lying here, in this glorious silkiness – even the air in this expensive room was silky – he would have been writhing in pleasurable anticipation, if he could have been bothered to move his legs. Perhaps, if he put his mind to it, if he could stop thinking about work for a week, he could bring himself to fall in love with Susie. She was a good sort, straight down the line, she was a trouper, she'd stick by him. At the thought, he was overcome by a sudden deep affection for himself as just the sort of person one should stick by, and he felt a tear run down his cheekbone and tickle his ear. He couldn't quite be troubled to wipe it away. And no need, for walking across the room towards him now was Molly, Molly Lane! And some fellow in tow. Her pert little mouth, the big black eyes, and a new haircut – a bob – seemed just right. What a wonderful woman.

'Molly!' Clive managed to croak. 'I'm sorry I can't get up . . .'

'Poor Clive.'

'I'm so tired . . .'

She put a cool hand to his forehead. 'Darling, you're a genius. The symphony is pure magic.'

'You were at the rehearsal? I didn't see you.'

'You were too busy and grand to notice me. Look, I've brought someone to meet you.'

Clive had met most of Molly's lovers in his time, but he couldn't quite place this one.

Socially adept as always, Molly leaned over and murmured in Clive's ear.

'You've met him before. It's Paul Lanark.'

'Of course it is. I didn't recognise him with the beard.'

'The thing is Clivey-poo, he wants your signature, but he's too shy to ask.'

Clive was determined to make everything all right for Molly and put Lanark at his ease.

'No, no. I don't mind at all.'

'I'd be terribly grateful,' Lanark said as he pushed pen and paper towards him.

'Honestly, you shouldn't feel embarrassed to ask.' Clive scrawled his name.

'And here too please, if you wouldn't mind.'

'It's no bother at all, really it isn't.'

The effort of writing was almost too much and he had to lie back. Molly moved in closer again.

'Darling, I'm going to give you one little telling off, then I'll never mention it again. But, you know, I really needed your help that day in the Lake District.'

'Oh God! I didn't realise it was you, Molly.'

'You always put your work first, and perhaps that's right.'

'Yes. No. I mean, if I'd known it was you I'd've shown that thin-faced fellow a thing or two.'

'Of course you would.' She put her hand on his wrist and shone a little torch into his eyes. What a woman!

'My arm's so hot,' Clive whispered.

'Poor Clive. That's why I'm rolling your sleeve up, silly. Now, Paul wants to show you what he really thinks of your work by sticking a huge needle in your arm.'

The music critic did exactly that, and it hurt. Some praise did. But one thing Clive had learned over a lifetime was how to accept a compliment.

'Well, thanks a lot,' he yodelled through a whimper. 'You're too kind. I don't make much claim for it myself, but anyway, I'm glad you like it, really, thanks awfully . . .'

From the perspective of the Dutch doctor and nurse, the composer lifted his head and, before closing his eyes, seemed to attempt, from his pillow, the most modest of bows.

v

For the first time in the day, Vernon found himself alone. His plan was simple. He quietly closed the door to the outer office, kicked off his shoes, switched off his phone, swept the papers and books from his desk – and lay on it. There were still five minutes before morning conference and there was no harm in snatching a quick snooze. He had done it before – and it must be in the paper's interests to have him on top form. As he settled he had an image of himself as a massive statue dominating the lobby of Judge House, a great reclining figure hewn from granite: Vernon Halliday, man of action, editor. At rest. But only temporarily, because conference was due to start and already – dammit – people were wandering in. He should have told Jean to keep them out. He loved the stories told in pubs at lunchtimes of the editors of old; the great V.T. Halliday, you know, of Pategate fame, who used to conduct his morning conferences *lying on his desk*. They had to pretend not to notice. No one dared say a thing. *Shoeless*. These days they're all bland little men, jumped-up accountants. Or women in black trouser suits. A large gin and tonic did you say? V.T. of course did that famous front page. Pushed all the copy onto page two and *let the picture tell the story*. That was when newspapers really mattered.

Shall we begin? They were all here. Frank Dibben, and standing next to him – pleasant surprise – Molly Lane. It was a matter of principle with Vernon, not to confuse his personal and professional lives, so he gave her no more than a businesslike nod. Beautiful woman, though. Smart idea of hers, to go blonde. And smart idea of his to take her on. Strictly on the basis of her brilliant work for Paris *Vogue*. The great M.L. Lane. *Never tidied her apartment. Never washed a dish.*

Without even propping his head on his elbow, Vernon started in on the post-mortem. Somehow a pillow had appeared under his head. This one would please the grammarians. He had in mind a piece written by Dibben.

'I've said this before,' he said. 'I'll say it again. A panacea can't be used of one particular illness. It's a universal remedy. A panacea for cancer doesn't make sense.'

Frank Dibben had the gall to come right over to Vernon. 'I happen to disagree,' the deputy foreign editor said. 'Cancer can take many forms. A panacea for cancer is a perfectly good idiomatic use.'

Frank had the advantage of height, but Vernon remained supine on his desk to demonstrate that he was not intimidated.

'I don't wish to see it again in my newspaper,' he said calmly.

'But that's not my main point,' Frank said. 'I'd like you to sign my expenses.' He had a sheet of paper in his hand, and a pen.

The great F.S. Dibben. *Raised his expenses to an art form.*

It was an outrageous request. In conference! Rather than stoop to argue, Vernon pressed on. This also was for Frank, from the same piece.

'This is 1996, not 1896. If you mean deny, don't write gainsay.'

It was a matter of some disappointment to Vernon that Molly should approach now to plead Dibben's case. But of course! Molly and Frank. He should have guessed. She was plucking at Vernon's shirt sleeve, she was using her personal connection with the editor to promote the interests of her current lover. She was bending over to whisper in Vernon's ear.

'Darling, he's owed. We need the money. We're setting up together in this sweet little place on the Rue de Seine . . .'

She truly was a beautiful woman, and he had never been able to resist her, not since she taught him how to roast porcini.

'All right. Quickly. But we must get on.'

'In two places,' Frank said. 'Top and bottom.'

Vernon wrote 'V.T. Halliday, editor' twice, and it seemed to take him half an hour. When at last he had done he continued with his remarks. Molly was rolling up his shirt sleeve, but to ask her why would have been yet another distraction. Dibben too was still hanging around Vernon's desk. He couldn't be bothered with either of them just now. He had too much on his mind. His heart raced as he found a higher oracular style.

'Turning to the Middle East. This paper is well-known for its pro-Arab line. We shall, however, be fearless in condemning, um, atrocities on both sides . . .'

Vernon would never tell anyone about the scorching pain in his upper arm, and that he had just begun to grasp, though feebly, where he really was and what must have been in his champagne and who these visitors were.

But he did interrupt his speech and fall silent for a while, and then at last murmured reverentially.

'It's a spoiler.'

vi

That week the Prime Minister decided on a Cabinet re-shuffle, and it was generally reckoned that despite the tide of public opinion running in Garmony's favour, it was *The Judge*'s photograph what did for him. Within a day the ex-Foreign Secretary discovered, in the corridors of Party headquarters and down among the backbenchers, that there was little appetite now for his November challenge: in the country at large the politics of emotion may have bestowed forgiveness, or at least tolerance, but politicians do not favour such vulnerability in a would-be leader. His fate was the very obscurity the editor of *The Judge* had wished on him; Julian Garmony was therefore able to make his way to the airport VIP lounge, to which his recent status still afforded him access, unencumbered by state papers and unattended by civil servants. He found George Lane pouring himself a Scotch at the free bar.

'Ah Julian. Join me, won't you?'

The two men had not seen each other since Molly's funeral and shook hands warily. Garmony had heard rumours that it was Lane who sold the photographs; Lane did not know how much Garmony knew. Garmony in turn was uncertain about Lane's attitude to his affair with Molly. Lane did not know whether Garmony realised just how much he, George, despised him. They were to travel to Amsterdam together to escort the coffins back to England, George as an old friend of the Hallidays and as Vernon's sponsor on *The Judge*, Julian, at the behest of the Linley Trust, as Clive's advocate in Cabinet. The trustees were hoping the ex-Foreign Secretary's presence might expedite the paperwork that dogs the international dispatch of a corpse.

They carried their drinks through the packed lounge – most people were VIPs these days – and discovered a relatively empty corner by the door to the lavatories.

'To the departed.'

'The departed.'

Garmony thought for a moment, then said, 'Look, since we're in this together, we may as well get it out the way. Was it you who supplied the pictures?'

George Lane drew himself up a useful inch and said in a pained tone, 'As a businessman I've been a loyal supporter and contributor to Party funds. What would be in it for me? Halliday must have been sitting on them, waiting for his moment.'

'I heard there were bids for the copyright.'

'Molly assigned the copyright to Linley. He might have made a few quid. I didn't like to ask.'

Garmony, sipping his Scotch, reflected that *The Judge* was bound to protect its sources. If Lane was lying, he did it well. If he wasn't, then Linley and all his works be damned.

Their flight was called. As the two were going down the stairs to the waiting limousine, George put his hand on

Julian's arm and said, 'You know, I think you came out of it bloody well.'

'Oh really?' Without seeming to, Garmony moved his arm away.

'Oh yes. Most men would have hanged themselves for far less.'

An hour and a half later they were being driven through the streets of Amsterdam in a Dutch government car.

Because they hadn't spoken for rather a long while, George said airily, 'I hear the Birmingham première has been postponed.'

'Cancelled actually. Giulio Bo says it's a dud. Half the BSO refuse to play it. Apparently there's a tune at the end, shameless copy of Beethoven's Ode to Joy, give or take a note or two.'

'No wonder he killed himself.'

The bodies were being held in a little mortuary in the basement of the main Amsterdam police station. As he and Lane were being led down the concrete stairs, Garmony wondered if there was a similar secret place beneath Scotland Yard. He would never find out now. The official identifications were made. The ex-minister was drawn aside for a discussion with Dutch Interior Ministry officials, leaving George Lane to contemplate the faces of his old friends. They looked surprisingly at peace. Vernon had his lips parted slightly, as though he were halfway through saying something interesting, while Clive had the happy air of a man drowning in applause.

Soon Garmony and Lane were being driven back

through the city centre. Both men were lost to their own thoughts.

'I've just been told something rather interesting,' Garmony said after a while. 'The press have got it wrong. We all have. It wasn't a double suicide at all. They poisoned each other. They had each other drugged with God knows what. It was mutual murder.'

'My God!'

'Turns out there are these rogue doctors here, pushing the euthanasia laws to the limits. Mostly they get paid for bumping off people's elderly relatives.'

'Funny that,' George said. 'I think *The Judge* ran a piece on it.'

He turned away to look out of his window. They were passing at walking pace down Brouwersgracht. Such a pleasant, well-ordered street. On the corner was a spruce little coffee house, probably selling drugs.

'Ah,' he sighed at last. 'The Dutch and their reasonable laws.'

'Quite,' Garmony said. 'When it comes to being reasonable, they rather go over the top.'

Late in the afternoon, back in England, having settled the business of the coffins at Heathrow, and passed through customs and then spotted their respective drivers, Garmony and Lane shook hands and parted, the former to spend more time with his family in Wiltshire, the latter to call on Mandy Halliday.

George had his car stop at the far end of her street so he could walk for a few minutes. He needed to plan what he would say to Vernon's widow. But instead, as he strolled through the cool and soothing dusk, past ample Victorian villas, past the sounds of the first lawnmowers of this early spring, he found his thoughts turning pleasantly in other directions: Garmony beaten down, and trussed up nicely by his lying wife's denials of his affair at her press conference, and now Vernon out of the way, *and* Clive. All in all, things hadn't turned out so badly on the former lovers front. This surely would be a good time to start thinking about a memorial service for Molly.

George reached the Hallidays' house and paused on the front steps. He'd known Mandy for years. A great girl. Used to be rather wild. Perhaps it was not too soon to ask her out to dinner.

Yes, a memorial service. St Martin's rather than St James's, which was favoured these days by credulous types who read the sort of books he himself published. St Martin's then, and he alone would make the speech, and no one else. No former lovers exchanging glances. He smiled, and as he raised his hand to touch the doorbell, his mind was already settling luxuriously on the fascinating matter of the guest list.